THE

Finding

of

Freddie

Perkins

First published 2013 by
A & C Black, an imprint of Bloomsbury Publishing Plc
50 Bedford Square, London, WC1B 3DP

www.bloomsbury.com

Copyright © 2013 A & C Black
Text copyright © 2013 Liz Baddaley
Illustrations copyright © 2013 Paul Fisher-Johnson

The right of Liz Baddaley and Paul Fisher-Johnson to be identified
as the author and illustrator of this work has been asserted by them
in accordance with the Copyrights, Designs and Patents Act 1988.

ISBN 978-1-4081-8608-4

A CIP catalogue for this book is available from the British Library.

Printed and bound by CPI Group (UK) Ltd, Croydon CR0 4YY

1 3 5 7 9 10 8 6 4 2

MIX
Paper from
responsible sources
FSC® C020471

THE

Finding

of

Freddie

Perkins

Liz Baddaley

Illustrated by Paul Fisher-Johnson

A & C BLACK
AN IMPRINT OF BLOOMSBURY
LONDON   NEW DELHI   NEW YORK   SYDNEY

'...for nothing is lost that can not be
found again if sought.'
(Edmund Spenser, *The Faerie Queene*)

Written for, and dedicated to, Jilly Bean
for Christmas 2010 – and for so many reasons.

Contents

1 Arriving nowhere slow 7

2 Then and now 19

3 Granny P speaks 25

4 Up and above 35

5 Some lovely finds 50

6 On the table 62

7 Out of the attic and into the house 69

8 The silence moves in again 79

9 The impossible might just be possible 90

10 In writing 98

11 Scientific observations 107

12 Find and seek 118

13 Seeing the full picture 127

14 More Fynd studies 133

15 Finding and keeping 144

Chapter 1

Arriving nowhere slow

It took Freddie Perkins exactly thirty-seven seconds to decide he hated Willow Beck. And another thirteen until he was sure, once and for all, that Granny P was as old, dusty and boring as her house was.

You might think this hasty or rash, but Freddie had had a lot of time to plan, and to consider what his reaction was going to be. He had formed it during all the endless thinking time he had had over the four months when he was packing up his room. He had perfected it whilst watching other children look at his awesome view over the London sky-scape. And he had confirmed it over and over again during what must surely have been a hundred-hour journey up endless motorways, with the red removal lorry following them and his mostly-silent dad driving next to him – all the way from Westgate Square Gardens to wherever it was in the middle of nowhere they were now.

* * *

It had been simply the worst year in history. And Freddie reckoned Dad agreed – even though he didn't say so.

It had started with the accident. That bleak January morning when the car was slower than ever to start and the brakes made that nasty squeaking sound that Mum always said was like a chipmunk stuck in a washing machine. It had been a freezing day, where playtime felt like punishment on the frozen playground and lessons seemed to go on forever, and then suddenly Freddie was pulled out of class and he felt joy in a rush at the freedom and then – a sickening despair when he saw the expression on Mr Grimthorpe's face.

There had been a phone call, apparently, and Dad was coming to fetch him to explain. At least, that was what Freddie thought he remembered Mr Grimthorpe saying. But it was difficult to recall the exact events through the fog that still seemed to surround his memory of that afternoon, and the weeks that followed. There had been a loud rushing like sea in his ears that started almost as soon as his headmaster started speaking, and did not stop until well after the polite-but-embarrassed conversations over dry sandwiches that stuck in his throat.

It was then, when he felt able to hear clearly again, that Freddie noticed the silence.

Mum had gone and in her place was silence.

But the silence was bigger even than the hole Mum had left behind. It seemed to take Dad's place too. He was still there, of course. But not *as* there as the silence was. It was in every room. Every conversation. It was the deafening sound of what wasn't said; a thunderous roar that shouted, over and over again, *Nothing you say will ever make things better now.*

Gradually the silence took over so much of Westgate Square Gardens that the only part of it where there was any air left to breathe was his room. He and Mum had spent hours up there last winter, carefully painting the famous London buildings you could see, if you stood on tiptoe to the right of the window, onto the back wall in mirror image. *Though Mum doesn't need to stand on tiptoe of course*, Freddie thought.

Didn't need.

He mentally corrected himself. Again.

Didn't need. She *was* tall. She *used to be* tall. No, it was no good. It still didn't sound right.

After school every night that winter, Mum and Freddie had sat at the kitchen table, chatting and laughing over steaming hot chocolate with sweets as floaters and extra sprinkles. And then they would go upstairs, find another building, and work out how to paint it shape by shape. Domes were semi-circles, and towers combined rectangles and triangles. Freddie's mum painted beautiful pictures. But better still, she knew just how to help him to see things like she did – shapes, colours and ideas.

They made up stories together, too. Amazing ones that made you believe the impossible was true. It all seemed so easy with Mum. But now he couldn't see any of it any more.

And so he sat in his attic bedroom, where the silence didn't dare come. And he looked at the wall. And he stood on tiptoe and stared out of the window, straining to see anything else to add to the wall. But there was never anything of course – because they had found everything last winter. And even if there had been something new, he wouldn't have been able to paint it now anyway. So it was pointless.

* * *

Freddie's dad had stopped coming up to his room so often from quite soon after the accident. When he did come, he seemed to bring the silence with him anyway – so Freddie didn't much mind that they didn't play computer games together any more, or shoot hoops over the waste bin, or have tickle fights. It was better to be on his own if it meant the silence stayed away.

To begin with, they had both tried to be out of the house as much as possible so they could escape it. And during those first few horrible weeks, when everyone thought it would be best if there was no school for him and no work for Dad, they had tried to find their old easy rhythm of chatter at all their favourite Saturday afternoon haunts.

But it seemed like everywhere they went together, the silence came too. It would sit between them at the cinema, no matter how funny the film had looked from the trailer; or sidle up to them in the queue for ice-cream at Scoops. It would rudely interrupt any excitement at a new exhibition at the Science Museum and it even seemed to muscle in on a kick-around in the park.

It seemed like it wanted to be there whenever and wherever Freddie and his dad were together. And eventually, if Freddie was honest, he started to be relieved when he sensed it approaching. It had become more familiar to him now than the polite small talk they made, or the sickening breathless feeling that came on him suddenly whenever his dad tried to start a conversation about 'things that mattered'.

So Freddie was almost pleased when the normal routine of school and work started again, and he got to stay in his room more, and to shut the door on it all.

After that, Freddie didn't know where his dad went to get away from the silence, because he didn't say, but it was definitely out. And it was definitely alone.

* * *

After a few short months that seemed more like an eternity, Dad decided that Westgate Square Gardens was too crowded for them. That was how it felt, anyway.

Other people said yes, of course they should move, because there was 'too much space' – it was such a big house for them to rattle around in, just the two of them.

And in a way they were right, Freddie supposed. After all, no one was using the studio any more, or the office. And there were no more dinner parties with his mum rushing around stressed beforehand, but then bubbling over with sparkling laughter that drifted up the stairs all evening.

Freddie knew what Dad meant, though. It *was* too crowded. There was all the space the silence took up, of course. But Dad said it was the memories that finally squeezed them out of the house.

Freddie thought it wasn't memories either, exactly. Instead, it was almost as if Mum needed more space now. Neither of them dared to put away anything she had left out anywhere, or settle down with the TV or a book in any of the rooms where she had done those things.

So Freddie agreed with his dad. The unspoken truth was acknowledged between them. They couldn't go on with their lives at Westgate Square Gardens without her. And as they *were* without her – horribly without her – they would have to leave.

Or at least Freddie had *thought* he agreed... until he knew the solution Dad had in mind.

* * *

The last weeks at Westgate Square Gardens became the last weeks in London. So there had to be a last week at school; a last day in the playground; and a last play round at Robbie's house. Then there was a last after-school hang out at Mrs Cook's next door while Dad worked late in the City for the last time, and a last stroke of her dog Fudge.

The lasts went on and on – endless lists of them that became so long Freddie simply couldn't hold them all in his head any more.

The lasts were bad. But this was worse.

They were *here*.

Miles and miles away from London – nowhere. Literally right in the middle of it. In a totally different country. At Willow Beck. With Granny P, who they never used to see much because she lived so far away, and was too old to make the journey down from Scotland often.

Granny P who wasn't at all like Grammie.

Grammie was chatty and funny and had dimples just like Mum's. She lived in Brighton, and Mum and Freddie used to catch the train to see her all the time until the worst year in history started.

Grammie had come to London on that horrible polite Thursday of course, and made all the sandwiches whilst Dad and he just sat there waiting for it to be over.

Freddie had been to stay in her bright beach house during the Easter holidays and half terms too. Even though it had felt strange without Mum, Grammie had been just the same, and there was no silence in any of her rooms. Each time, Freddie came back desperate to see Dad, imagining somehow that he would now be who he was before the accident. But each time he wasn't, and so Freddie would find himself wishing he could have stayed with Grammie for longer.

Granny P was quiet and spoke in such a whisper that she made it even harder for you to understand her strange accent. And she was definitely not funny. She had no dimples – in fact she wasn't at all the same shape as Grammie, who was like a giant marshmallow, and gave you such fiercely wonderful hugs that you were torn between never wanting them to end and being desperate to get your breath back.

Granny P was skinny, bony and frail. She looked like she was made of wrinkly, folded paper that would crumble into a thousand tiny pieces if she ever chose to give you more than her customary brief, delicate embrace. She wore old person clothes, too. Flowery dresses, pastel cardigans, and starchy, tweedy suits. Not like Grammie's flowing, colourful clothes or sparkly, bright jewellery.

And she had never bounded up to Freddie's room to play computer games, look at his skyline mural, or shoot hoops, like Mum, Dad and Grammie. Instead she sat quietly on Mum's favourite paisley chair, drinking tea and talking in her strange quiet tones to Mum – who seemed bizarrely riveted by every word she uttered between her tiny, fairy-like sips.

And so the thought Freddie had had, or rather the thousands of thoughts he had had over and over again, as they travelled up endless motorways to *live* with her at Willow Beck, had understandably been: 'This is unquestionably, undoubtedly, going to be the most perfectly horrible ending possible to the worst year in history.'

* * *

In the fifty seconds since Dad had parked their car outside Willow Beck, got out, rung the doorbell, and been greeted by Granny P in her usual fragile way, Freddie had been able to swiftly conclude that all his thorough and careful predictions over the last few months had been right.

Willow Beck was a large, imposing building, rising up almost as if it had grown itself out of the stones already there around it. The house was grey, and surrounded by equally grey, craggy rocks that were its only company on top of the steep hill it stood on. Freddie quickly counted the windows stacked up the far left hand side of the building through the window of the car where he still sat. There were four... then across, five – one for each gable – and every one was dark and lifeless-looking.

The door was huge and wooden, and Granny P, standing in the massive chasm left by its opening, looked comically dwarf-like. She was half in shadow because the light from the hall behind her was dim, making almost no impression on the dusky half-light surrounding the house.

Freddie sighed, swallowed tears in his now expert fashion, and bravely pulled the handle back just as Dad looked towards the car as if to gesture it was time for him to come. Freddie got out, his legs heavy and reluctant on the stone driveway, and walked slowly to the front door. His dad put an arm round him and together they followed Granny P into Willow Beck, the huge oak door slamming shut behind them with depressing finality.

Chapter 2

Then and now

It seemed like weeks ago, but actually when Freddie counted carefully it was only last Tuesday that they had arrived at Willow Beck.

Time went slowly here. As slow as the solemn grandfather clock in the gloomy hall whose pendulum seemed to limp as it swung to and fro, to and fro in its monotonous dirge; as slow as Granny P climbing the stairs carefully and creakily one at a time – in fact, sometimes Freddie wasn't sure whether it was the stairs that were creaking, or Granny P herself.

Freddie decided to spend this rainy Saturday morning making a list in his head, reciting everything that was different, and horrid, about Willow Beck compared to Westgate Square Gardens – in the old days before the silence, that was.

His mind drew up two columns of opposites. It was dark, not light; cold, not warm; and full of old, dark things rather than bright colours. The chairs were hard, upright and dark, not all sinky-in-to and cushy like the big squidgy ones in the snug at home. Or like that massive one in Mum and Dad's room which he used to fall asleep in when he insisted on 'staying up' to watch cartoons when he was ill, or lonely, or a bit frightened after a bad dream.

There was nothing to do here, no friends nearby to see, and nowhere to go. And sometimes, even though he was very rarely frightened in normal circumstances, Freddie had to admit that he found the wind circling the house at night as terrifying as the cry of someone in pain.

In fact, he had to remind himself that it was just the wind. Night after night, tense and breathless, he would edge along the corridor to Dad's room and pound on the door. But Dad seemed to fall asleep before he did now, and so Freddie would lie next to him – comforted enough not to be frightened, but still lonely, listening to the wind moan on and on around Willow Beck.

* * *

The worst thing about life here was how positively, adamantly, insistently and totally convinced his dad was that Freddie was going to *love* Willow Beck just as soon as he got used to it. It was like an endless repetition of the same play that they performed every day at some point between half two and seven o'clock that whole first week. Every day it was the same – the only thing that changed was how long Dad would wait before commenting on his 'moping'.

He would urge Freddie to 'just come on', assure him that he knew how tough it was leaving all his friends and blah blah blah; insist that he was sure Freddie would love it here if he just gave it a chance.

Dad droned on and on about how he had always wished that Granny and Grandpa P had had this house when *he* was growing up. And how, when he had come for tea with Great Granny and Grandpa McCormack, who had lived here when he was young, he had spent the whole time wishing he would just be allowed out of the drawing room to explore and explore. And then of course he would start going on about all that space outside. And... blah blah blah.

Apparently Freddie would 'see'; he would 'come around'.

But Freddie didn't see and was certain he wouldn't come around. He had heard this mantra so many times now, right from the first mention of moving to Willow Beck, and he remained completely unconvinced. His dad's memories and descriptions of the house, which his parents had inherited from Great-Granny and -Grandpa McC whilst he was at university, didn't seem to match the house Freddie knew at all.

His dad painted a picture of mystery, magic and excitement, as if behind every heavy oak door was a whole world of ancient treasure maps, secret passages and false panels.

But Willow Beck was not one of those houses you read about in stories – there was nothing magical about it. And certainly nothing mysterious, unless you counted why anyone would want to live there in the first place. Or why on earth they would want to collect and keep such a boring, dusty array of dark old wooden furniture and faded ugly knick-knacks.

And all that space outside that Dad seemed so excited about was grey, wild and cold. Even in July! Besides, what could Freddie possibly do with the space? There was no playground or hoop, and the steep slope of the garden, down seven or eight different levels of hill to the rough, gorsy fields below, was no good for kicking around his football.

Freddie concluded there were two options: either Willow Beck was totally different then, or something was seriously wrong with his dad's memory. Perhaps life in Lochside village had simply been so boring that even a trip to Willow Beck had seemed exciting.

But Freddie didn't see how that could have been possible, even then. Perhaps Dad was just trying to trick him into liking the house. Perhaps he thought Freddie would stop complaining about living there if he believed it was a house of secrets.

Well, Freddie was way too smart to fall for that. He wasn't going to explore the house's every corner hoping to find hidden passages, secret turrets and magical treasures. He wasn't that kind of kid.

Not any more.

He knew now that none of that stuff was real – least of all at Willow Beck. Freddie wasn't going to play along with some fairytale scheme to make Dad think he was happy and excited, however silent and sad Dad was these days.

Freddie didn't even want to try to hide the fact that he was desperately remembering *then*: Westgate Square Gardens on any day of the week, with hot chocolate, and painting – and Mum.

Chapter 3

Granny P speaks

By the following Thursday the three inhabitants of Willow Beck had settled into an uneasy rhythm with each other.

Freddie had more than four long weeks left to somehow fill in the big, empty house, before school would start. He didn't know how he would survive it. Time went so slowly here, and it was so dull.

Not that he wanted school to start either. Not here.

On the previous Monday, Dad had started his new job in Glasgow. He left too early for Freddie to summon the energy to turn over and check the clock when he came in to say bye before making the long drive in time for his nine o'clock start. Dad didn't get back until seven in the evening. So for most of the day it was just Freddie and Granny P in the house, except for two hours on Tuesday when Mrs Quinn came in to clean, seeing as how Granny P was too old to manage most of the proper housework. (Though Mrs Quinn seemed almost as ancient, and very nearly as frail, as Granny P herself.)

Granny P and Freddie ate a silent breakfast together at eight; a silent lunch at half past twelve; and a silent tea at fifteen minutes past six.

At least the quiet at Willow Beck meals was different to the silence at Westgate Square Gardens. It had less to do with a threatening, *other* presence, and more to do with the length of the oak dining table in the dining room, the state of Granny P's hearing, and her generally reticent manner. She always sat at one end, and at that very first meal they ate together, Freddie had made a point of sitting at the opposite end – as far away as possible – and so that was where Granny P now laid his place.

When Dad was there, he would sit at the side of the table, half-way between them, and attempt to make stilted conversation both ways, like a polite interpreter introducing two alien tribes.

But when Dad wasn't there, there was quiet. And instead of talking, Granny P spent the whole meal very still – smiling at Freddie in between taking tiny mouthfuls and then chewing them very slowly.

Freddie didn't mind the quiet with Granny P, since it wasn't awkward, and because if she were to speak to him for any length of time, she would doubtless do what all adults did now. She would start by asking him lots of questions about how he was feeling, and then tell him how wonderfully *brave* he was.

Freddie hated those conversations.

Granny P was boring, old, quiet and frail, but at least he didn't have to talk to her.

Between meals they went their separate ways. Granny P usually spent the morning in the garden room or the library. Freddie didn't know what she did in these rooms, but whatever it was, it was always quiet. In the afternoons she would potter round the house slowly, going in and out of different rooms on the second floor, dusting, polishing and cleaning everything she touched gently and lovingly – even the very ugliest things in the house. Freddie knew this because he saw her doing so sometimes through the open door of his room.

That was where Freddie spent most of *his* time. In his room. Sometimes he'd go outside and kick his ball around at the front of the house where the drive was flat, but mostly he stayed in his room, surrounded by his stuff, and able to think occasionally that not absolutely every last thing had changed.

* * *

But on Friday, at lunchtime, the meal didn't follow routine.

Halfway through her bowl of soup, Granny P looked at him for a bit longer than usual between mouthfuls. That was the first strange thing.

Next, she put down her spoon entirely.

Then she uttered such a loud and long sigh that Freddie was quite scared for a moment that she was seriously ill. But with surprising strength she stood up, slowly pushed her chair under the table, and then walked round the side of the table towards him.

She came right up close until their faces were no more than a few centimetres apart, looked him in the eyes, and then moved away to slowly pull across one of the side chairs – making a screeching noise with it on the floor – until she could sit very close to him.

She sat on it. And then she spoke. Even though Dad wasn't there. Even though there was nothing specific to check on, she spoke.

'Freddie,' she said in her whisper of a voice, 'I've stayed quiet out of respect. But I have to speak now. I'm not going to ask you to talk about anything you don't want to. And I'm not going to assume anything about who you are now, how you're feeling, or what you think about this ghastly year. But we are going to talk about one thing...'

Freddie's heart was beating fast. Granny P had gently taken his hand as she started talking, though he had barely noticed till now, and whilst her little speech had been strangely comforting at first – it felt like she *understood* somehow – he was beginning to feel nervous. What was she going to talk to him about? Was he in trouble?

'... and that is the attic.'

'The attic?' said Freddie, before he'd had a chance to decide whether he was going to talk to Granny P or not. 'The attic? Why would we talk about that?'

'Because I need help with it, Freddie,' she whispered, 'lots of help. I want to clear it out. I've had a look at what's up there, and even with help from Mrs Quinn, I'm not sure I can manage all the lifting, carrying and sorting myself.'

Freddie didn't want to be mean, but he felt that was the biggest understatement he had ever heard.

'Will you help me, Freddie?'

'Um... I... well,' he stuttered.

It was not that he didn't *want* to help, exactly – he quite liked helping people. It was not even that Granny P was old and boring, because she was OK, really. But if they were doing something together, they would have to talk, wouldn't they? And what would he talk to Granny P about? Would she be trying to get him to talk about *things*, after all?

But there was nothing he could say without being rude.

And without getting into trouble with Dad.

And anyway, he got the feeling that even if he had it in him to be rude to Granny P – which he didn't – she wouldn't take no for an answer. She looked stronger and more determined than he had ever seen her before... almost bigger.

'Sure.'

'Oh, that's excellent, Freddie. Thank you. There really is so much to do. I cannot put it off any longer. We must begin right away – as a matter of urgency.'

And with that, she stood up, moved the chair back with the same screeching sound, and walked out of the room, leaving her soup half-eaten, and a sense of unfinished business behind her. Freddie frowned. Where was she going? Did she mean this afternoon?

But it became apparent that Granny P did not mean that afternoon, or any part of that weekend – even though Dad was away, back clearing up the last bits of the sale of Westgate Square Gardens, and not due back until late on Monday night. Freddie was at a loose end, and more bored than ever, having had the week entertaining himself alone, and now the weekend – but Granny P didn't say anything more about the attic.

* * *

By Monday lunchtime, Freddie was so fed up, and so intrigued as to why Granny P had made such a point of speaking about the attic, only to then return to silence, that he could wait no longer.

'Granny P,' he said.

There was no response.

'Granny P?'

Freddie sighed and put down the teaspoon he had been about to bash his boiled egg with. He hesitated. Then he got off his chair and walked down the long side of the table towards Granny P, sliding Dad's chair noisily along until he, and it, reached her side. He sat down again.

Granny P looked up and smiled. 'Freddie!'

Freddie had never noticed before quite how much her small form lit up when she smiled. She seemed overjoyed – luminous almost. Was that all because he was sitting by her at her end of the table?

After a few moments of beaming at him, Granny P returned to her eggs.

'Granny P?' Freddie asked again.

'Yes, dear?'

'I was wondering...'

'Yes, dear.'

'When were you wanting to start on the attic? I mean, when did you want me to start helping you with all that work you said there is to do?'

'Why as soon as you're free, dear,' said Granny P, 'because I'm really anxious to begin. But I didn't want to interrupt what you've been working on so busily in your room. When do you think you might be available?'

Freddie did a double take. He'd assumed they had been waiting for Granny P. No one apart from Mum had ever talked to him as if he had things to do that mattered. Well, that mattered to anyone but him, anyway. And actually, since coming to Willow Beck, and maybe even longer – since the accident – he didn't feel like he'd done anything that mattered even to him.

He felt a bit guilty. Granny P had clearly thought he was drawing or something. And he'd not really been doing anything – just sitting around being bored.

'I, oh, I... what I mean is, I can probably take a break from what I'm doing. I've just been... well, I... I could even start this afternoon.'

'Freddie, that is so kind of you. But I don't want you to drop everything just to help me. We'll do it when you're ready.'

'But I *am* ready, Granny P. I... I'd like to help this afternoon.'

'Well, why ever didn't you say so?' said Granny P with another beaming smile. 'We'll begin just as soon as you've eaten up your eggs – go on with you.'

Freddie hadn't thought she'd noticed that he hadn't eaten his eggs. Maybe she missed a bit less than he had realised.

Chapter 4

Up and above

Freddie had decided to count the number of stairs they were climbing to get to the attic, because he imagined it would be an impressive number. But somewhere after twenty-five he lost count in the round and round of it all, and the concentrating on not treading on the backs of Granny P's slippers as she went up ahead of him to show him the way, and the sheer endless slowness of her pace.

Freddie thought it was quite funny that she insisted on going first, especially given that she was so slow, and there was surely only one way up once you had opened the door on the landing at the bottom of the attic stairs. But for some reason, it seemed to be important to Granny P.

When they reached the top of the stairs – well, when Granny P reached the top of the stairs (Freddie was still stranded a couple of steps below her, unable to move until she entered the attic space) – she paused for a few moments to catch her breath, which she seemed to be in surprising need of, despite the slow pace of her wheezing, creaking ascent. Her shallow breathing went on for so long that Freddie wondered if he should say something or check she was alright. But then, suddenly, she said, 'Well then Freddie, come on, don't be dawdling down there – we've got work to do.'

And Granny P was forward, unlocking the door with a big old-fashioned key, the kind you never see now, and then through into the attic.

'Turn on your torch, Freddie,' instructed Granny P.

'It always takes a while for me to find the light switch up here.'

Freddie shuffled into the darkness behind Granny P as he fumbled with the torch... and then suddenly, a bright beam of light sprang out, and the darkness seemed to open up a little to his eyes as he moved the beam around in front of him.

There were chests, boxes, piles, and several mysterious shapes hiding under sheets – and they were all crammed together in what felt like an impossibly small space. It wasn't until Granny P found the switch, and two or three slightly swinging light bulbs came on, that Freddie saw that the attic was in fact a huge, cavernous area.

They were in the eaves of Willow Beck, and from the front of the house there were five gables. The attic seemed to run the length of all five, and though Freddie could see nothing but stuff in the one they were standing in, he could tell that they were in one by the shape of the ceiling above them, and the outline of four more – two to the left, and two to the right. He also knew that, despite the spiralling round and round of the stairs, they must be facing forwards, out towards the front garden and the approach to the house, because the pointy bits were in front of them.

Now, peering further through the still dimly lit space towards the gables, Freddie made out first one, then two, three, four, five faint thin glimmers of daylight, somehow penetrating the thick layers of grime and dust. Windows! Freddie could hardly imagine how far you would be able to see through them.

We're so high up here, he thought. *You must be able to see for miles.*

He felt a twinge of sadness, but as Granny P was already poking around various items in their current section, he pushed it down, and determined to help her. She was so small and frail. And there was so much stuff!

Besides, there was a faint sense of adventure building in him. Being up here in the half-light, you could almost imagine that you might find treasure after all, in the old attic of the house where four or five sets of Great-Great-Greats had lived before even Granny P's parents.

'Now, Freddie,' said Granny P, 'no one has sorted this attic in the longest time you could possibly imagine. Once when I was a wee lass, younger than you for sure, your Great-Granny McCormack and I spent an afternoon up here with the intention of starting. She was looking for something in particular, I think; but she decided it was too much trouble, and she wouldn't leave me to do it on my own.

'So for at least my lifetime and hers, and possibly even longer, McCormacks and Perkinses have been coming up here, adding more and more things, but never taking the time to look at what is behind the latest batch of "saving for a rainy day".

'Freddie, if we can really do it – you and me – if we can sort through all this stuff in the next month, I'm sure we will find some incredible things.'

Freddie was a little slow in answering Granny P's obvious pep talk, because his brain needed to catch up a bit with all the possibilities.

'You mean we might find things that have been in the attic for a hundred years, Granny P? Or even longer?'

Granny P chuckled at Freddie's wide eyes and wonder-struck tone.

'I knew you'd understand, Freddie,' she said. 'I knew you'd understand.'

Freddie knew it had reached four o'clock because even all the way up here he could hear the chimes from the massive grandfather clock in the hallway.

He couldn't believe how long they'd been up there. Mostly they'd just been chatting. Freddie had asked Granny P why she'd not sorted the attic in all these years since she'd come back to Willow Beck and it was hers to decide about, and when she got that look that told you an adult was going to give you a long answer, Freddie had told her to wait a minute whilst he had searched for something for her to sit on.

He'd found something remarkably easily – right near the front, where he'd not noticed it before, was an old chair – and with a bit of wriggling past awkward, spiky obstacles he brought it into the small open space near the door to the stairs.

Granny P sunk gratefully into it with a little wink and a chuckle, and Freddie perched on the arm to listen.

Then Granny P told him about how, when she was young, she used to imagine all the things that were up in the attic, but that after that time Great-Granny

McCormack had talked about sorting, she had never done so again, and though Granny P had asked every summer holiday if she could do it herself, she was never allowed.

She explained that when she and Grandpa P had moved into the house after Great-Granny McCormack had died, she kept thinking she would do it at the first opportunity that came. But somehow she didn't.

'Freddie, I don't expect I can make you understand. But when we moved into Willow Beck, I began to feel like I didn't want to change anything in the house. I didn't want to move things that my mother had decided to put in a particular place for whatever reason – even if I didn't know what that reason was, and even when it was the last place on earth I would have put something – I wanted to have it there because she had had it there. Silly, really.'

Granny P paused, and Freddie wondered whether he should say that he understood completely. He didn't think it was silly at all. But he didn't feel quite ready, and the words stuck in his throat.

'And then it was just me not so long after that, and I did want to change things then. Maybe I didn't want just memories. I don't know. But the attic always seemed too much to tackle on my own.

'And so it's just been here, waiting... for a rainy day, or a brave day, or perhaps just a day when I had a friend who would enjoy it too.'

And with that Granny P smiled at him again, and the clock downstairs brought them back to the present with four chimes.

'But Freddie, it's four o'clock! Good job I brought up some provisions.' She chuckled, and produced a couple of slightly squished muffins.

Freddie laughed. 'Where were you hiding those, Granny P?'

Granny P patted a pocket on her dress that he'd not realised she had. 'It might seem silly to you, Freddie, but I only ever wear dresses with pockets. You never know when you're going to need supplies,' she said conspiratorially.

This time Freddie could speak.

'Oh, I understand that, Granny P!' And with that he dug down into his lower left leg zipped pocket and produced two similarly squished toffees. 'Pudding,' he announced.

Granny P just laughed, and laughed, and laughed.

* * *

That first afternoon in the attic was strangely magical. As Freddie sat listening to Granny P's soft voice, and watching her wrinkled face come alive with laughter, memories and possibilities, he found himself transfixed. He got caught up in her stories, and more than that, he began to see through the wrinkles to the real Granny P inside.

He could almost imagine her now as a little girl, her blue eyes full of the same kind of wonder that they were full of now.

And it made him understand why his mum had gravitated towards her, happy to simply sit and listen, on those rare occasions when Granny P had visited Westgate Square Gardens.

It figured. Freddie's mum had loved stories too, and pictures, and anything that made you imagine things in your mind.

And though it made Freddie sad to remember his mum, it felt strangely safe to do so in the stillness of his heart as they sat there in the attic – which itself was a place where memories went to live.

* * *

When they got round to beginning the actual sorting it was about half past four, but it was amazing what they found in just a couple of hours.

Freddie made Granny P laugh when he tapped her on the shoulder to model how he looked in a slightly too-large-for-him top hat, and Granny P pretended to be a posh lady when she found a fox scarf and a lacy fan. They found vases, bowls, and old ugly ornaments that Granny P said might be valuable, so they put them aside to ask Dad to take them to Edinburgh to be valued.

There was even a small leather case full of old money, carefully sorted into different categories, which Granny P said straight away was the sort of collection they should keep in the family, and that she could think of no one better to look after it than him.

Freddie felt strangely proud.

They found old wooden toys, including a beautiful old rocking horse which Granny P said was hers when she was a child, and Freddie experienced a twinge of regret that he was too grown up for it. But then he laughed, because she said exactly what he was thinking, and the thought of today's Granny P sitting on the rocking horse was just so funny.

It was strangely comforting that they had thought the same thing about something they had found. They agreed it would be nice to have the rocking horse in the drawing room in place of a cabinet full of ornaments that Freddie now discovered Granny P thought were ugly too.

* * *

About an hour into the actual sorting, Freddie was sat cross-legged looking at a pile of illustrated atlases and travel books, when a muffled cry from Granny P, whose head, shoulders and arms were all buried in a huge wooden packing crate, interrupted him.

'What did you say, Granny P?'

Granny P giggled as she emerged. 'Sorry, Freddie. I said there's something at the bottom here that I just can't reach. It's so dark in here, I can't even see what it is.'

Freddie smiled at her. 'Let's see if I can get it,' he said.

Together they managed somehow to lay the tall crate down, and then Freddie was able to crawl in on his hands and knees, edging forward one elbow at a time. When he'd got as far in as he could, he switched on the torch, and blinked against the brightness it created in the small enclosed space. There was something wedged right into the corner, but even with the torch he couldn't see what it was, because it was wrapped in some kind of fabric.

Freddie felt a bit like a champion potholer, or a miner exploring for diamonds, or maybe even an archaeologist on a dig in some ancient, tomb-like passage.

It was fun being so close to getting it, but it was no good, he couldn't quite reach it...

He was beginning to edge back the way he'd come, when Granny P's voice again interrupted him.

'Try this, Freddie. I used to play for the school, you know.' And she slid a lacrosse stick gently into the space next to him.

Freddie grasped the lacrosse stick, and edged forward once more, being careful not to bang his head on the top of the crate. He slid it out in front of him, breathless and hot by this point, and hooked it into the corner and around whatever it was that was trapped there.

'I've got it! I've got it!' he cried, hugging it to him excitedly, and jerkily crawling back out of the cavelike space with his treasure – the lacrosse stick left behind and forgotten.

Freddie flopped into one of the chairs and started to unwrap layer after layer of fabric, the object feeling harder and spikier in his hands as he did so, until with a flourish he uncovered it, and Granny P gasped.

'Oh Freddie, it's beautiful!'

The teapot in his hands was heavy and ornate, and covered with a raised thistle design. On its spout were trailing leaves which they couldn't quite identify, and a small but stately bird which Granny P said was a miniature golden eagle was perched on its handle. Freddie could see from just the first glance that it must be valuable, and when Granny P showed him how to check the bottom for a hallmark, they discovered it was solid silver.

'Wow, Granny P!' said Freddie. 'This is amazing. It's like a genie lamp!'

'Oh, you're right, Freddie. You'd better polish it carefully in case something magical happens.'

Of course nothing did happen when Freddie polished it, but it was fun to pretend it might, and as he sat and rubbed it clean with the silver cloth, he took to imagining what three wishes he would choose to make, but it was so hard to choose. Well, all except one, of course.

* * *

Granny P disappeared into a dream world of her own when she found some old photographs of their family. She wanted to point out everyone she could make out to Freddie. By then, though, he was too distracted by a locked, battered chest he had found in a corner when he was looking for somewhere to temporarily display the genie teapot. But even when he finally managed to prise Granny P away from the faded brown pictures, and her colourful memories of the people in them, they couldn't get the heavy wooden lid to open. There was no key anywhere obvious, and neither of them was strong enough to force it open.

Granny P said they would ask Dad to force open the chest – that she didn't mind if it got a bit more battered in the process. They simply *had* to know what was in it.

In fact, both of them were so distracted by the mystery of the locked chest that they couldn't concentrate much more after that. They did manage to move enough stuff out of the way to clear and bring forward a large dining table, which Granny P said would make the sorting so much easier when it was fully folded out. Tomorrow they would be all set, as they could put boxes and bags on it, and then organise things into piles in front of them.

Freddie then spotted a couple of chairs that matched the old table behind a wardrobe, and so with one final effort, they managed to squeeze them round it. With the chairs now in front of the table, they had created a proper sorting station to continue their work tomorrow.

Exhausted, they descended for supper, Granny P with the photos to pore over by the fire, and Freddie with the genie teapot tucked under his arm to put on his bedside table on the way downstairs. Granny P had said he ought to keep rubbing it every now and then just in case, and although Freddie knew that the glint in her eye was just for his benefit, he decided to go along with it. After all, it meant he could keep the teapot in his room, and somehow it did feel a little bit magical to have something like that next to your bed – even just for pretend.

Chapter 5

Some lovely finds

After that afternoon, the routine at Willow Beck changed. Not gradually. Not with any discussion or planning. Suddenly, and dramatically. And it started with dinner that evening.

Freddie and Granny P couldn't stop talking to each other – laughing about what they had found, and coming up with weirder and weirder ideas about what might be in the locked chest with no key.

It was slow going at first because every time Freddie said something, he had to repeat it three or four times until he was practically shouting – just so Granny P could hear it at her end of the table.

But halfway through his stew, Freddie put down his knife and fork and stood up. He moved his chair to Granny P's end of the table so they were sat close enough to talk normally and then he said, 'Granny P, I'd like to sit here for all my meals now.'

Granny P didn't say anything. She just smiled – such a smile, it looked like it was too big for her small, wrinkled face.

And breakfast the next morning was the same. They took a long time over it because they were chatting and laughing away to each other.

Freddie couldn't understand why Granny P seemed so different all of a sudden, and so easy to talk to. Had she changed? Was she just excited about the attic? Or had she always been like this, but he had never really noticed before? It was a mystery.

But not as much of a mystery as that locked chest. Granny P said that she too had taken ages to get to sleep last night wondering what on earth was in it. Dad had got home from work very late last night – long after Freddie had finally fallen asleep – and so they hadn't been able to get him to open the chest then.

But today was Wednesday. Dad had a day off after all his late nights and so he would be able to do it – they would know what was in the chest! Freddie was all for waking Dad straight away and marching him up to the attic immediately, in his pyjamas if necessary, so they could open the chest. And he said so. But Granny P insisted they let Dad have a lie-in after such a tiring week.

'Freddie, here's a plan. You go up first and begin with some of those boxes of newspapers we saw in the far left gable. I need to sort a few things down here first, so you start without me. I'll let your father sleep a bit longer, take him his breakfast in bed, and then when he's feeling rested – and grateful! – bring him up to tackle the chest.'

Freddie jumped straight up. Yesterday afternoon had been amazing. And the new Granny P was super improved and really quite fun. But the idea of going up to the attic by himself was *irresistible*.

He was very practical about it. He had no notions of finding something properly magical up there – that kind of thing only happened in stories. But he might be the one who found something truly valuable. It was absolutely, practically possible – likely even – that there could be something incredible up there, given how old some of the stuff was. And if there was, he *so* wanted to be the one to find it.

Freddie heard Granny P chuckling as he sprinted out of the dining room and up to the attic. It was almost like she knew, like she'd planned it this way and found some things to do so he would have the thrill of going up alone – just like she had longed to do when she was younger. And that made Freddie laugh too.

This time the ascent to the attic was much quicker. He took every flight of stairs – even the spiral one up to the attic – two steps at a time, and by the time he reached the door into the attic, his heart was pounding from the effort and excitement of it all. Granny P had left the key in the lock, and the torch next to the door, so in no time at all he was in. He switched on the lights, surveyed the marvellous scene, and shut the door behind him.

He let out a long, happy sigh. He felt so different up here that it was like being in another world, a world where there was a possibility of good things happening again.

He puffed his chest out and tried to do his best hale and hearty pirate impression.

'Longbeard – aargh – shiver me timbers but there's a good lot of treasure here.'

Not bad, he thought. A bit rusty. But then, he hadn't done it for a while.

He was swaggering over to the corner to find the boxes Granny P had mentioned when suddenly a glint on the sorting table caught his eye.

He walked back towards it, suddenly reverting to the role of Freddie Perkins.

'No way! Absolutely no way! Awesome!'

For there on the table was a key.

And something inside him simply knew it had to be *the* key. He rushed over to the chest and tried it in the lock. A perfect fit! And though it was a bit stiff from being closed for so long, the key turned. Now he could finally see what was inside.

His heart pounding, Freddie was about to open the chest when suddenly he remembered Granny P.

It wouldn't be fair to open the chest without her. He desperately wanted to look right now, but something in him was strong enough to resist. He didn't want to be unfair to his new friend – after all it was her attic, her chest, and the sorting had all been her idea.

But of course it was now impossible for him to wait until Granny P and Dad came up to the attic in their own good time. That would be unthinkable. He held the key tightly in his hand, put his clenched fist into his pocket – just to be sure there was no chance of losing the precious object – and ran all the way back down the stairs to find Granny P.

But in the hall, another thought struck him. In all that excitement he had not considered how the key had got there. Yesterday they didn't find any keys at all. Today there was a key on the table. Exactly the right key. Just there on the table. Waiting for them. Or, waiting for him, because of course he had gone up alone.

He had been *sent* up alone.

Freddie figured it out in a flash.

Granny P was just like all the other grown-ups after all. She was playing a game with him. She'd obviously known where the key was all along, sneaked back up to the attic after he was in bed, and put it out on the table, before locking the door and putting the torch back in its place, ready for him to find when she sent him up on his own the next morning.

No doubt she was going to try to convince him there was some kind of magic or haunting going on in the attic.

Freddie was disappointed. And he was angry, too.

He had thought they were sharing an adventure, that he was really helping... that they were in it together. But now it felt like a big let-down, a conspiracy to cheer him up – as if a stupid attic could ever do that.

Well, two could play at that game.

Freddie ran back upstairs.

He would lock the chest again and hide the key. He would call Granny P's bluff.

And of course he would look in the chest himself now, before locking it again and pretending to be none the wiser.

* * *

It was probably about half an hour after he had first gone up when Freddie heard Granny P and Dad coming up the stairs. They were talking to each other about the mysterious chest, and Freddie thought that Granny P would surely not be playing a trick on his dad too. But then he realised they must have planned it all together, and their conversation now was really for his benefit – a little charade to further build his sense of excitement.

'I know it seems silly, Stephen, but really I didn't get a wink of sleep for thinking about it. Whatever could be inside? Of course it's probably something terribly dull, and it's just made exciting by the mystery. I hope we won't all be dreadfully disappointed.'

'Don't resolve it all now, Ma,' said his dad. 'I haven't got it open yet and I may not even be able to.'

'Ah, sure you will, lad,' said Granny P, 'after that hearty breakfast I gave you, too.'

'Slave labour and bribery.'

'Well, don't you catch on quickly?' said Granny P. Freddie could hear the chuckle in her voice. And then they were in.

Dad and Granny P both seemed so excited about the chest, and pleased to see him busy sorting already. And Granny P was really delighted with the progress he had made on the boxes full of old newspapers.

Some of the front page headlines were amazing. Freddie had started putting them in order, and the earliest one he had found so far was from 1888 – imagine!

Freddie felt a bit unsure whether or not he had done the right thing about the chest. But he said nothing – and kept turning the key over and over in his pocket to be sure it was still there. He felt even more confused when Granny P didn't mention it at all – not even when his dad ended up bruising his hand with the crowbar he was using to try to prise open the chest.

But then, Freddie didn't mention the key either.

Still, Granny P was an adult. Adults stopped games when they went too far, didn't they?

Freddie was wondering whether to pretend he'd just found the key before Dad seriously hurt himself, when with a cry of excitement, he got the chest open.

'Freddie, come quickly!' shouted Granny P. 'It's open!'

Freddie feigned excitement swiftly followed by disappointment. 'Oh, I don't believe it,' he said. 'It's empty.'

Granny P looked like she might cry. 'I'm so sorry,

Freddie,' she said, 'I shouldn't have let us get so excited. I feel awful now. I was really hoping there would be something amazing in there for us to find together.'

'Let's all go and have a cup of tea,' said Freddie's dad to the two despondent faces in front of him. 'I'm sure you will find lots of exciting things up here. You just need a bit of a time out, like all good teams do. Come on.'

And with that they all went downstairs, shutting the door behind them.

Granny P turned the key in the lock and gave it to Freddie. 'I know this doesn't make up for it, but I think you should be the key-keeper. You're doing such a brilliant job with the sorting, Freddie. I hope we do find something remarkable somewhere to reward all your hard work.'

* * *

They had some of Granny P's shortbread with their cup of tea, but Freddie found it stuck in his throat a bit.

Granny P seemed genuinely disappointed – as disappointed as he would have been if the chest had actually been empty.

But of course it hadn't been.

Freddie had only had time to quickly flick through the diaries he had found in there. But he knew they were seriously old, very valuable and potentially full of amazing stories. From the initials on the front, and the various photos stuck inside them, he knew that they were written by one of his great-great grandfathers on the McCormack side of the family – one of Granny P's grandfathers or great-grandfathers probably. But he'd need Granny P to tell him which one. And he was still deciding whether he would 'find' them in front of Granny P or not. It might not matter knowing exactly whose they were, or he might be able to work it out eventually from dates and events – he knew already it was one of his great grandfathers that had done a lot of exploring, so a few well-placed questions might trick Granny P into giving him the answer he needed without her finding out why he was really asking.

But for now, while he decided, the diaries were safely hidden further back in the fifth gable.

Hang on, though. Did Granny P already know he had the diaries?

The more he thought about it all, the more

confused he was. Surely Granny P would be cross, or at least anxious to know where such precious things were. Her behaviour now suggested she didn't know what had been in the chest. But if she hadn't known, it didn't really work as a set-up, did it?

Why would she have pretended there was no key, but had the key and put it out for a chest whose contents she honestly didn't know about? It was all very strange. The more he considered it, the more he thought Granny P genuinely had been as excited as him – that maybe she hadn't known about the key. But how was that possible?

Someone had put the key on the table.

Freddie didn't understand how it was possible, but he was definitely starting to have some doubts about whether Granny P had been involved. He decided that he would 'find' the diaries again. But he felt the weight of something not very nice pressing down in his mind. Even then he would be lying to Granny P. And he didn't feel quite so angry any more.

He tried to tell himself that it would be just the same for Granny P if he 'found' them now, after their tea break. But of course he knew it wasn't.

Chapter 6

On the table

When the three of them went back up, Freddie got out the attic key. He had been a bit nervous that he'd produce the wrong one and get found out, so he'd been reciting to himself *left is chest, right is attic* all the way up the stairs to be sure he didn't get flustered and forget.

It was Granny P that spotted them first.

The diaries were on the table – neatly stacked in the middle.

Freddie was genuinely dumbfounded.

He had hidden them in the far gable, quite far back and well out of sight; he had been the last person in the attic; and he had the only key. Even if there was a duplicate which Granny P had not let on about, Freddie had been with her and Dad the whole time since they had come down from the attic.

The diaries were not there when they left. No one had been back up. And they were there now.

Granny P was ecstatic about the new find. And so was Dad.

'Freddie, come here, this is really something,' said Dad.

'To think,' said Granny P, 'we were so fixated on that silly chest that we missed what you were sorting through – and that you'd found these with the newspapers. Freddie – you've found something truly special! I'm so sorry we didn't notice straight away. Didn't you realise what they were?'

By now Freddie was so confused that he had a genuine look of bewilderment about him – he had no need to pretend anything. He was truly baffled. Search as he might through every possibility, he simply couldn't find any rational explanation for how those diaries had ended up on the table.

'But they weren't here. There was nothing on the table before.'

'Oh, Freddie,' said Dad, ruffling his hair, 'you must have been away with the fairies when you were looking at those newspapers, and totally missed the diaries sitting under them.'

'I didn't miss them. They weren't here,' repeated Freddie, and then quietly again to himself. 'I *know* they weren't here.'

'Oh come on, Freddie, they didn't just appear out of nowhere. We're not falling for that one. Nice try.'

Freddie wanted to protest, but he knew there was no point. He couldn't explain it, and even if he tried he'd have to admit his part in finding and hiding the diaries. It would just have to be another thing between them that he let go.

* * *

Well, of course, once the diaries were discovered, especially because Dad was at home, the attic was abandoned for the day and they all sat round the dining room table poring over them together.

And so Freddie did find out the answers to his questions. The diaries belonged to Great-Great-Great-Grandpa Walter Seymour McCormack. They were more than 150 years old, which in itself was quite astonishing. They detailed W.S. McCormack's explorations in Egypt, and talked about the people, the land, and the artefacts that he had discovered.

It was incredible, thought Freddie. His great-great-great-grandfather had been like an ancient Indiana Jones!

But, fascinated as he was, Freddie was distracted. He couldn't fully enter into the excitement that Granny P and Dad felt, and that he would have felt, had not the diaries appeared on the table after he had hidden them somewhere else.

It niggled and niggled at him until he could bear it no more.

Whilst Dad and Granny P continued to decipher and read the first of the diaries, Freddie slunk away from the table. He decided to go back up to the attic. Just to see. Would there be anything else on the table?

This time Freddie felt nervous opening the door by himself. But he took a deep breath, turned the key and found the light switch without even using the torch.

There was nothing untoward. Nothing on the table. Nothing different to how they'd left it. He felt relieved mostly, but also a tiny bit disappointed. But why would there be anything? It wasn't like he had actually been expecting something to appear out of nowhere... had he?

Freddie backed away from the table, and feeling a little silly, and still more confused, edged his way out on to the landing, closing the door of the attic behind him.

He locked the door and went back downstairs.

* * *

At the end of the day, after reading the diaries all the way through until late into the evening, Dad, Granny P and Freddie agreed they needed to be kept somewhere really safe. They decided the attic would be the best place – that way they could be kept locked away, and out of the light which might be damaging to them.

In fact, Granny P said, the ideal storage place for them would be in the empty chest.

So they all climbed up again, to put the diaries away safely until they could speak to the curator at the local museum.

When they opened the door and went in again, it was Freddie's dad who spotted it.

'Look!' he said, pointing to the table in surprise.

On it was a beautiful necklace. Even in the half-light of the attic, it was sparkling brightly as the swinging bulbs cast their slightly shimmering light over it. It was gold, with a number of large green stones surrounded by clusters of what Freddie thought must be diamonds.

'Well, how beautiful, and how valuable this must be,' said Granny P. 'We must take it into Campbell and Sons as soon as we can. But where did it come from? Freddie, did you find this too?'

'No,' said Freddie. 'It wasn't here when we came down with the diaries. The table was empty.'

'Hmmm,' said Freddie's dad. 'I smell a rat. First the diaries, and then the necklace. Freddie, are you playing a game with us?'

'No, I'm not,' said Freddie. 'If anyone's playing

games, it's not me. I didn't put the necklace there. It wasn't there when we left.'

'Well, no, sure, not when *we* left. But I heard *you* come back up, didn't I? You must have put it on the table then. Very good, Freddie! A great find, and a clever joke too to try and make us think it had just appeared.'

'I'm not playing any jokes,' said Freddie.

'Now, Freddie,' said his dad, 'I let it go earlier with the diaries, but this kind of thing isn't funny. I understand you're just trying to have a bit of fun, and cheer us all up, but these are valuable objects and they're not yours. You should be treating your grandmother's belongings with much more care. Playing around with things this precious is irresponsible and I don't want to have to tell you about it again.'

'I'm not playing around with anything!' protested Freddie, doubly annoyed by the accusation and his dad talking as if he were a little kid. And he went to bed without even saying goodnight.

Chapter 7

Out of the attic and into the house

Freddie felt confused, isolated and cross. Why didn't Dad believe him? Who was playing tricks? And if no one was, how on earth did the diaries and the necklace get on to the table when no one had put them there?

Even the excitement of the diaries couldn't distract him from his persistent, worried wondering. What was going on at Willow Beck?

By eleven o'clock that night the whole house was quiet. But Freddie's thoughts were so loud they kept him awake.

Scary though it was, he resolved he must go up to the attic again. Now. Tonight. On his own.

Maybe there would be more clues this time. Maybe something else would be on the table. Dad and Granny P were both in bed, and no one had been up since the necklace was found, so if anything had changed this time, he'd know for sure that something weird was going on.

It was surprisingly cold for a July night and so Freddie pulled on a thick jumper and some socks and then quietly opened his bedroom door to creep first past Dad's door, then Granny P's, then up the stairs, and up again, and up and round and round – until he finally reached the attic.

Slowly, and as quietly as he could, Freddie turned the big old key in the stiff old lock until the door opened. And as he gently switched on the light he saw a sudden movement as something leapt off the table and behind the boxes underneath it. Perhaps a tail...

Freddie started. It was all he could do not to scream.

He wasn't frightened of mice – and he was pretty sure that was all it was. But even so, late at night, in the dark, and alone in the attic, it was a bit more than he'd bargained for.

He ran back down the stairs, two at a time where he could manage it, terrified he would wake everyone, but petrified by his now heightened awareness of all things crawly and night-like.

He bolted back to his room, dived under the duvet, and lay tense and breathless until he gradually realised that no one else had woken up, that he was after all quite safe, and that it was probably only a mouse he had seen – or imagined.

It was then that he remembered that he hadn't shut the attic door. And that the key was still in the lock from when he opened it. His stomach turned over. He didn't want his dad to know he'd been up there, and jump to conclusions about what he was doing there alone and at night. He pulled back the covers to get up and go back, but it was no good, he had spooked himself good and proper and could not face it. There was nothing for it. He would simply have to get up before the others and sneak up and put everything right.

* * *

But when Freddie woke up the next morning – with a start – it was to realise that the sound that had woken him was Granny P clanging things around downstairs. When he looked at his clock he realised he had overslept to such a degree that she might already have been up to the attic.

His heart sank.

And then he saw it.

Poking out from behind the clock, where he'd be sure to see it, was the attic key.

It wasn't possible. But there it was.

Before he could even begin to think about what another strange appearance meant, there was a knock at the door and Granny P followed it with a tray of tea and crumpets, and a beaming face. She was humming something to herself, and soon explained why.

'Freddie, the most wonderful thing has happened.

And I thought we simply must have crumpets in bed to celebrate.'

'What's happened?'

'This morning I found my wedding ring. I lost it when I was cleaning a few weeks ago and I was devastated. But this morning I found it, sitting right behind my alarm clock. How I didn't see it before I don't know. But I'm just thrilled to have found it again.'

Freddie looked at the attic key, just visible behind his own clock, and thought to himself that it sounded rather more like the ring had found Granny P than that Granny P had found the ring. But that was ridiculous, so he told himself to stop being so silly.

'That's great, Granny P,' he said, biting into a crumpet, and then licking the extra splurges of honey from his fingers, 'that's really great.'

* * *

When Granny P and Freddie went up to the attic after breakfast they found it locked as usual, and Freddie rubbed his eyes, wondering if he had, after all, dreamed getting up, opening it, and leaving the key behind.

But he knew deep down that he hadn't dreamed it at all.

And there were other signs that things had happened during the night. There were no new treasures on the table, but there were some small pieces – looking almost as if they had been a bit chewed – of the yellow scrap paper that he had thrown away during yesterday morning's sort. And though he was aware that he might be imagining it, he was pretty much convinced that several things were in slightly different places to where they had been at the end of yesterday afternoon.

Granny P and Freddie made good progress that day, finding a few more collections that Granny P said Freddie should keep, and a few things she said might be valuable. Perhaps the best find was a music box made from burnished walnut. Granny P said that should definitely be out for them all to enjoy, like the rocking horse they had found on the first afternoon.

They worked so hard, and Freddie was so tired, that it was well into the evening, after supper, before he noticed that a few things had changed around the house whilst they had been in the attic. In fact it was Granny P who spotted the first one.

'Oh look, Freddie, look, my photo of Reg – your Grandpa – on the day we first met. It fell down behind that big bureau a few months ago and neither Mrs Quinn nor I was strong enough to move it out so that we could get the photo back. I don't remember mentioning it to your father, but I must have done. What a kind thing to do for me to shift that heavy piece of oak. Oh, I do so love to look at that photo and just remember...'

Then Freddie spotted two more in quick succession. Exactly at eye level from his favourite chair in the sitting room, on the third from bottom shelf of the big bookcase in the corner, was his MP3 player, which he'd mislaid last week... upstairs.

And the hat trick was literally that. His dad's baseball cap, which he'd been moaning about losing, was on one of the coat stand's hooks in the hall.

Once Freddie started looking for changes, he found them everywhere. A set of three small glass animal ornaments had become four, a number of the smaller items of furniture had moved slightly to the left or right, and a five-pound note was sitting, bold as brass, in the spare change dish in the hall.

* * *

When Dad got home around eight-thirty, he stepped through the door, and noticed his hat straightaway.

'Oh, brilliant! Who found my cap? Where was it?'

When there was no response, Dad came into the sitting room, where Freddie and Granny P were relaxing companionably, chatting over the day's amazing finds between sips of marshmallow-laden, piping hot cocoa.

'Hi, rascal,' he said, ruffling Freddie's hair and then crossing the room to kiss Granny P on the cheek. 'Where did you find my hat?'

'I didn't,' said Freddie.

'Oh, was it you, Ma? Where was it?'

Granny P looked up, 'I don't know, Stephen. I didn't find it. Freddie, are you sure you didn't find it somewhere, and then just forget?'

'No, I didn't. I have no idea where it came from.'

'Now, Freddie,' said Dad, warningly. 'I hope you're not starting to play games again, are you?'

'No!' said Freddie angrily. 'I've already told you both. I don't know where it was and I didn't find it. Why does nobody ever believe me? Why are you being so stupid?'

'Freddie!' snapped his dad. 'How dare you speak to your grandmother and me like that!'

Freddie felt crushed by the injustice of it all. He didn't know what was going on at Willow Beck, but he knew one thing. *He* wasn't behind it. He tried to hold his anger in, but he couldn't. It was bursting out in a rush.

'I hate you! Why do you never listen to what I say? Why don't you ever believe me?' he shouted, and with one final whimper, 'Mum would have believed me.'

At that point he caught Granny P's eye, and he felt ashamed. He knew he wasn't being fair on Dad. But Dad wasn't being fair on him either.

Again he went up to bed without saying goodnight. Only this time, he was sent. And as he climbed the stairs, feeling painfully alone, he heard his dad say, 'I'm so sorry, Ma. I guess I should have expected that he would play up. He misses her so much. I thought you were getting through to him, but I think he's just withdrawing even more with all this hiding and pretending. I don't know what to do.'

'Give him time Stephen. Give him time,' said Granny P, softly.

Freddie tried to swallow the lump in his throat. He did miss his mum. And all the time since the world began wouldn't change that. But he hadn't been hiding and finding things. Why would he want to do that?

After all, it would never bring back what was really lost.

Chapter 8

The silence moves in again

Freddie's door slammed behind him with a crash in perfect synchronisation with his dive on to the bed. But all the noise in the world couldn't have drowned out the shouting in his head.

It's so unfair! It's all just so unfair!

And then suddenly out of nowhere, the rushing noise in his ears was back, and the tightness in his chest, and the rising tears that never quite made it but stuck halfway up his throat and made him feel like he was choking.

And there was a new feeling too – an anger so big he felt like it must belong to someone else – a huge angry giant perhaps. No wonder it felt like he couldn't contain it in his boy's body. He hated all these feelings, and the fact that he seemed powerless against them, but most of all he hated that no one else seemed to have them.

In fact, he hated everyone and everything.

* * *

After a few minutes, when the giant's anger seemed to reduce slightly and it was easier to breathe, Freddie was able to sit up.

He looked around him desperately for comfort. Was there anyone or anything that would understand how lost and lonely he felt?

Freddie reached for the genie teapot and held its solid, spiky realness close to his chest, wrapping his arms as tightly round it as possible – not even caring about the pointy silver thistles and the golden eagle's sharp little beak. He knew it was stupid but he screwed his eyes up and wished that she would come back.

Wished and wished and wished with all his might. All three wishes used up on just one thing – the only thing that mattered.

But of course nothing happened.

And then there was a knock on the door, and Granny P's soft tones were entreating him. 'Freddie? Freddie? Can I come in, Freddie?'

Freddie didn't answer. He was still too angry to speak. And he didn't want Granny P here. Not now. Possibly not ever.

The door creaked open nevertheless, and Granny P came slowly into the room and sat on the end of the bed. He could see her kind eyes taking him in: his tense clenched body, and the teapot spout poking out from under his right arm.

He realised she knew what he'd been doing and he didn't like it. He didn't like her knowing at all. And he didn't want to hear whatever adult cheering-up lie was coming next.

He wouldn't hear it. He *wouldn't* listen to it! He didn't have to take any more of their pep talks and understanding words and kind gestures and clever tricks and... and accusations.

'Get out!' he shouted. 'I don't want you here. I don't want any of you. I didn't say you could come in. I don't want you here. I only want Mum. Just Mum. You don't understand. I don't want your stories and your games and your cheering up. I don't want *you*!'

And then, with a final defiant 'Go away!' he threw the teapot at the door.

It made a huge clang and then lay there awkwardly, propped up by its handle with its lid thrown back half unhinged. Freddie looked at it and hated it too – it was almost as if it was laughing at him through its wide gaping lid.

Granny P didn't say anything at all, but she looked shocked and sad and kind and hurt, all at the same time.

For the longest moment she continued to sit and wait.

But Freddie wouldn't do it; he wouldn't break the silence with an apology.

Eventually, she slowly got up, picked up the teapot, whose lid would now not properly close, and put it back next to Freddie.

And as she did so, he saw it – a tear that she hadn't been able to keep in was rolling down her cheek.

Freddie felt suddenly panicked. He didn't know what to do. He hadn't meant to damage the genie teapot; and he hadn't meant to hurt her – well, not really anyway.

He felt alone and confused and out of control.

But just as he was trying to think what to do, his dad came running up the stairs and into his room. He must have heard the crash of the teapot hitting the door, and now his outraged eyes took in the scene in Freddie's room. Granny P silent, sad, and on the verge of more tears; the damaged teapot on his bedside table; and Freddie's defiant, hunched body, scowling from the bed.

'Frederick!' he shouted. 'What has got into you? This is no way to behave. I'm so disappointed in you. This is not how you were raised. I had to warn you yesterday about hiding valuable things, and today you're deliberately destroying your grandmother's precious belongings! This is an appalling way to treat her. And when she has been so kind to you!'

At this, Freddie looked at Granny P as if to appeal for help. Surely she understood a little bit. But his eyes only met her retreating back as she left Dad and him alone.

'I warned you yesterday about all this, Freddie,' his dad continued angrily, 'and now you're lying too. And being rude. I don't understand what you want. I don't know how to help you. I've tried talking about things with you; I've tried giving you space. But whatever you're playing at now, this is not the way to get attention. We all know things are hard but you are just making them worse for everyone. Think what Mum would say!'

The panic in Freddie's heart at Granny P's pained retreat had been growing and growing as Dad started to talk about Mum. He didn't know what was worse – the horrible false accusations… or the horrible truth.

Freddie could contain it no longer. He exploded with the only fight back he could think of that would end this dreadful awareness that Mum would be devastated if she could see him now.

'You can't tell me what Mum would say. No one knows what she would say. She isn't here. She's never coming back. And I know you wish it was me gone, not her!'

The moment Freddie said it, he knew he'd done something terrible.

He hadn't ever realised that words could have such an effect. All the angry red colour drained out of Dad's face at once; it went almost white; and his body, which had been so tense and angry, seemed to crumple in on itself. Every feature slumped with defeat and pain.

Dad opened his mouth to speak, but nothing came out.

Then, it returned. Into the space between them the silence rushed in, and as if sensing its presence had come even here to Willow Beck, his dad turned and left the room, with Freddie still sat on the bed, looking after him in horror.

* * *

Freddie sat in the same position until he got pins and needles.

And then he was forced to move and do something other than wonder how the last hour had just happened, and how the angry giant had so totally displaced Freddie Perkins, and how he would have normally acted.

He sought comfort in the only place it was to be found.

The large sequinned box under his bed had been Mum's, of course. It still smelt of that flowery perfume that she had loved and Dad had always teased her about. Sometimes, Freddie remembered, she had chased Dad round the room trying to squirt it on him, saying he could do with smelling a bit more of 'sissy flowers' himself.

Freddie smiled when he remembered that. If he concentrated hard enough he could almost hear her bubbling giggle, and then her shrieking laughter when the chase inevitably turned, and Dad would catch her, and tickle her until she cried out for mercy and promised to put the perfume away.

She used to smile at Dad in such a way, then. The way she would smile at Freddie. A smile that said, 'You are the centre of my whole world.'

Freddie wondered if his dad missed those smiles as much as he did, now that every time you so desperately needed one, you had to remember and imagine it out of nowhere, rather than getting a fresh one as a gift more times than you could count in a single day.

She was magical, his mum. Everyone agreed.

And even in these fleeting fragments of her life, kept in a box, some glimpse of that still remained.

With each precious card, note, photo or pretty object of hers that Freddie looked at, the silence retreated a bit more. As if somehow Freddie was leading against it an army of pink envelopes, hair clips, hastily scribbled love notes and sketches of flowers and trees and characters from his favourite books as Mum had imagined them from his descriptions.

Mum's things advanced against the silence, until eventually it left his room altogether and he could breathe, and think, and be himself again.

Right near the bottom, he came across a drawing he'd only seen once before – a delicate watercolour picture of a sandy-coloured creature set in a beautiful hand-carved wooden frame. Dad had found it when he was clearing out Mum's closet and had given it to Freddie. The creature in it was facing into the page, as if it didn't want to be seen, but its head glanced back slightly – just enough to reveal kind, wise eyes and the softest, friendliest face.

Freddie held the new sketch for quite a long time,

taking in Mum's talent again, and wondering what the creature was, and why Mum had drawn it.

He remembered the day Dad had found it, and how they had both treasured finding a fresh piece of her even then, when no more new things could be created. And he thought again, as then, how kind it was of his dad to give this new piece of his mum away.

He wondered again how his dad felt.

No more new paintings to marvel at; no more new ideas lighting up her face; and no more notes, hidden for Dad in his briefcase, or stuck to his shaving mirror, or (one time) placed at the bottom of his cafetiere.

Freddie smiled again at this memory. His dad had been so tired that Saturday morning, he'd just scooped coffee in and poured boiling water right on top of it, and his mum had laughed and laughed, and refused to tell him what it had said.

Of course she'd relented later when Dad had brought the shopping home with her favourite pink and white lilies nestled in among the baguettes she'd asked for. And then Dad had ruffled his hair, winked at him, and said, 'Remember that, rascal, flowers are a man's best weapon.'

Freddie thanked the old Dad in his head.

That was what he'd do.

He'd get up early, pick some flowers for Granny P, and find a way to say sorry, even if words wouldn't work.

But what could he do to show Dad he was sorry? How could he ever make up for the magic Dad had lost, and the fact that he, Freddie Perkins, who knew more than anyone else in the world how Dad felt, had said those terrible words?

His dad had been quick to accuse him, but he'd been just as unfair on Dad.

He fell asleep still trying to work out a solution, still in his clothes, and slept deeply, as if held down by the weight of everything said and unsaid and desperately needing to be said.

Chapter 9

The impossible might just be possible

The next day, Dad woke him up early to say goodbye before he left to drive to Glasgow.

Freddie was relieved because he had been worried that he would sleep through his dad getting ready, and that he would have already gone to work before Freddie could say sorry.

He did try to apologise.

'I... well, I'm... uh... really sorry about last night, Dad,' he stuttered, 'I... uh... didn't mean to...' And then he trailed off, at a loss how to broach the words he'd thrown at Dad in his desperation.

But his dad seemed reluctant to get into any of it; and he still looked crushed even as he awkwardly tousled Freddie's hair.

Although there was peace between them again, it was uneasy and polite. And of course Dad didn't apologise for any of *his* accusations, because he believed they were all true.

And so Freddie was still left feeling isolated and misunderstood, as well as guilty for his part in inviting the silence to move into Willow Beck.

He lay in bed for longer than usual after Dad had left, reluctant to get up and face a second round of awkward apologies with Granny P. But eventually, he knew, it had to be done.

It was better to face her in the neutral territory of the dining room than to have her come up here again, where the genie teapot would mock him – a misshapen reminder of what he had said and done to Granny P, who after all hadn't really accused him of anything.

* * *

On the stairs his feet seemed to drag behind him, rather than leading the way. And in the garden behind the kitchen, he took a ridiculously long time to pick some of the roses Granny P loved to bring into the house. He kept wondering, what would she say?

Freddie had two scenarios outlined in his head.

The first, and most likely, must be that Granny P would tell him off for last night, or perhaps try and get him to confess that he had put the diaries and necklace on the table, and the hat on the stand, after all. But there was also a chance that instead she would choose the option of pretending the whole thing hadn't happened. She might try to carry on as normal, perhaps deciding to chat about what they would sort that day in a slightly-too-cheerful tone.

But what Granny P actually did was a total surprise.

When he came into the dining room she smiled, and patted his chair, which was still next to hers.

'Freddie,' she said, 'come here and sit next to me. I want to apologise for your father – he always was one to assume everything has a rational explanation.'

'Well, it does,' mumbled Freddie.

'Not every time, Freddie. Not every time. Now, I have been thinking. I was up all night, trying to make sense of this conundrum we find ourselves in. Things are appearing that have been lost, and it's not me or your father. But I don't think that means it has to be you, either.

'I don't believe that you were playing tricks on us with the hat, the necklace, the diaries, or anything else that's gone missing or suddenly appeared. You have been so helpful to me, and I just don't believe you would be messing around with things that for the most part are very valuable and don't belong to you.

'Now, I know that last night got a bit hairy – especially for the teapot!' She gave a little giggle before continuing more seriously, 'But I was once falsely accused of something and I felt like the whole world had turned on me. It was the most horrible, panicky kind of feeling. And I'm guessing that was just a fraction of how angry you must have felt last night.

'So... some cross words, and a teapot getting caught up in the distress, seem fairly small fry to me. What is surely more important is sorting out what is going on at Willow Beck, so there are no more misunderstandings that get out of hand and become giant angry arguments.'

Freddie just looked at Granny P, dumbfounded. He wasn't in trouble *at all*? She wasn't disappointed in him? Or distant? Or at a loss for words?

She actually *understood*? About the angry giant and everything?

'What I'm saying is, I believe you, Freddie. I don't understand how things could be appearing out of nowhere. But perhaps I need to let go of understanding everything, because I know that you would not lie to me. We are friends. And the attic project belongs to both of us.'

This was too much for Freddie. Because of course she was right and he was so relieved. But she was also wrong – he had lied to her. And he felt terrible.

He felt his chin wobble a bit, and then before he even knew it was happening, the whole story came out: the key, the fact he had thought *she* had tricked *him*, opening the chest, hiding the diaries, the diaries appearing again, the empty table when he went back, the necklace... then the night visit, the open door, the locked door, the key by his clock, her ring by hers, and all the things that had shown up in the house since. It all came out in one jumbled stream that he was sure wouldn't make any sense.

Granny P just listened the whole time he was speaking, patting his knee almost absent-mindedly and looking at him with kind eyes throughout it all, so that even before she spoke he knew he wasn't in trouble.

'My dear Freddie, we are friends. We are sorting the attic together – *together*. I see how confusing it all has been and how it must have made you feel. But let me assure you I have not, nor will I in the future, play any kind of trick on you to make you feel like something more is happening than it is.

'There are enough unexplained things in the world without us creating more, Freddie. The excitement of what is true is so much more magical than anything we could make up ourselves. I am sad that you chose to open the chest without me. But I understand that was because you were struggling to believe that it wasn't a trick.

'But we must believe it now, mustn't we? For we need to solve it. Someone, or something, is bringing things to our attention – we are having things found for us. And as it isn't either of us playing jokes, and it isn't your dad, the only rational explanation is that something non-rational is going on.'

Granny P paused before continuing in a firm voice, as if she needed to convince herself as well as Freddie that she really believed what she was saying.

'Someone or something is living in the attic. Something good, because it's helping us.'

'But that's impossible,' sniffed Freddie.

'What other explanation can there be?'

'Well, I don't have one. But *that* can't be what's happening. The attic has been locked all these years. No person could be living up there secretly. And no mouse or anything could know what was valuable and lift it on to the table. It's impossible that there's something in the house finding things.'

'Irrational isn't at all the same as impossible, dear,' said Granny P, 'you'll learn that soon, for sure. Trust me, Freddie. Something is up there, and we are going to find out what. We must be careful though. We don't want to frighten it. I have a suspicion, in fact, and if I'm right we need to be *very* careful not to frighten it. Let me just get the right book...'

Freddie looked after her in puzzled disbelief for a moment, and then noticed that he was still holding the roses. He hadn't even needed them to convince Granny P that he was sorry. He smiled and put them down next to her plate for her to see when she returned.

Chapter 10

In writing

But when Granny P came back into the dining room she was carrying such a large book that she couldn't see past it to notice whether there was anything new on the table.

The book smelt faintly damp and musty and its pages were soft with use and age. Granny P put it on the table next to Freddie and opened it carefully. The title said *Creatures of Fell, Beck, Loch and Croft* in old curly writing.

'Your grandfather was always poring over this book, Freddie! He used to tell the most amazing stories of these creatures to your father, your mother, me... in fact anyone who would listen. I think we all had different opinions about what was made up, what he might actually have seen, and what he'd simply taken from this book. But there is one that is really coming to mind for our situation.'

Granny P carefully turned to the back of the book and ran her finger down the index entries. *Badger, Cornish sprite... elf, fox... Loch Ness Monster... mole...* and back up until it rested on *the Fynd*.

'That's it,' said Granny P, 'from what I can remember, Freddie, that's it. Page 279.'

Freddie looked at her in disbelief. From a glance through the index it appeared to be a book that contained as much fantasy as fact. It was ridiculous.

Granny P turned to page 279. And there it was, an entry written in factual and scientific language about 'the Fynd' – a creature allegedly indigenous and unique to Scotland, and very rare.

'Very rare. Well, yes, that would make sense,' said Freddie sarcastically. 'So rare, it lives in the head of one person who made it up, and then died hundreds of years ago by the looks of this book.'

'Freddie,' said Granny P, 'I have told you that this is the only rational explanation that I can think of. I agree that we shouldn't believe everything we read in books – but that also goes for serious books that act as if they know everything there is to know about the world, you know.'

Freddie pondered this for a moment. It was all like a riddle. But then, so were the mysteriously appearing items. His brain hurt a little, but with a sigh he decided he had nothing to lose from reading the entry.

* * *

Silly as the whole notion was, having read nearly seven pages on 'the Fynd', all Freddie and Granny P could do was stare at each other in wary, silent agreement.

Freddie read the summary out loud again:

> The Fynd is small, shy and generally apt to hide in cluttered places where it will not be noticed. It likes the indoors, where it is warm and dry, and where it can

surround itself with objects to sort and hide in or behind.

It likes to interact with humans, but from a distance – this interaction typically taking the form of finding and presenting objects which have been lost, or which are unknown to the humans present, but have some form of value, whether monetary or sentimental.

The Fynd's exact physical appearance is unknown since it so persistently hides itself, even when it has made its presence known to the humans it is serving. However, it is thought to have a long tail, as several partial sightings have glimpsed this sandy-coloured appendage protruding from the Fynd's hiding places.

It is thought to survive by eating small amounts of waste paper, which tend to be in plentiful supply in the places it selects as habitats.

It was discovered and named in 1601 by William Fynd.

'Granny P?' asked Freddie. 'Do you really think we could have a Fynd living in the attic? I mean, I can hardly believe such a thing exists. But do you honestly think they are real? Not just a silly thing someone made up?'

'Well, I don't know, Freddie. It seems implausible. But it's the best explanation we have. How do you suppose we could find out?'

Freddie shook his head. 'I don't know. But for now, let's not tell Dad. I'm not saying I believe it, but he *definitely* won't. So we should wait for some proper proof before we mention it to him.'

'Good idea, Freddie,' said Granny P. 'We mustn't jump to conclusions without evidence to back them up. After all, that's got us all into trouble recently, hasn't it?'

Granny P and Freddie sat in silence for some ten minutes, before Freddie had the idea. 'I think we should put out some paper for it,' he said, and he grinned at Granny P.

Granny P smiled too. 'Yes, that's a good idea. We'll put some paper out on the table in the attic and see if it disappears.'

So that was what they did.

At the end of that day's work in the attic, they left some paper out on the table. Freddie worked especially hard to choose different types of paper, and to tear them up into tiny pieces that he imagined might be more manageable for a small creature.

* * *

But first thing the next morning, when they checked before breakfast, the paper was still there. Freddie found himself oddly disappointed, and glancing across at Granny P he could tell she was feeling the same.

Then suddenly it hit him. 'Granny P, Granny P!' he shouted in excitement, jumping up and down. 'Of course there's no Fynd in the attic any more – it's in the *house!*'

There was a few seconds delay as Granny P caught up with that thought and put everything together...

Things in the main part of the house had started showing up the day before yesterday – the day after Freddie had left the attic door open.

'Yes Freddie, of course! You're right,' she giggled excitedly. 'When you left the attic door open, the Fynd must have got so excited at the chance to investigate the rest of the house – maybe it had even found all the most valuable things up there, and knew there would be things we had lost that really mattered to us in the house. It must have come out of the attic, locked the door behind it, returned the key and then got to work. So the question is, where in the house should we try leaving the paper?'

'Where else?' grinned Freddie. 'The dining room!'

Freddie and Granny P were so excited that they completely forgot their own breakfast, laying out a feast of paper scraps in place of their porridge, and then creeping out and closing the door behind them.

'How long should we leave it?' asked Freddie.

'Well, I think it wants to be friends,' said Granny P. 'So it might be confident to come and eat what it wants quite quickly... let's give it an hour.'

Neither Freddie nor Granny P was much good at being patient with a mystery. First one, then the other crept up to the dining room to listen against the door with a glass from the drinks cabinet in the drawing room. But they couldn't hear anything. And they certainly couldn't get on with anything else meanwhile. It was just impossible.

Freddie was getting so desperate after just twenty-five minutes that he was all for going outside, walking round the house, and peering in the dining room window, but Granny said they mustn't. They must have resolve, and a spirit of endurance.

And so, after what seemed like weeks, an hour had finally gone by and together they approached the door to the dining room. Having spent the last hour frantically wishing time forward, they were strangely hesitant at the threshold.

Granny P took a deep breath and pushed open the door.

There was just one piece of paper left on the table. A piece of newspaper carefully bitten around to leave just two words in print – 'thank' and 'you'.

And next to it, as if to underline its sentiment, was another key.

Granny P and Freddie looked at each other, wide-eyed and amazed.

Here it was. On the table in front of them. Proof. They had a Fynd *in their house*!

It was too wonderful to be real, but somehow it must be.

For a few moments they just kept looking at each

other, and then Granny P started to gently shake her head and say 'No, it can't be.'

But of course it *was*.

And as the truth settled into their minds it pushed out any remaining doubts that such a thing was not possible, and first Freddie, and then Granny P, began to giggle and clap, and laugh and dance. Well, Freddie danced; Granny P sort of bobbed and smiled, but her whole body seemed lit up with delight and excitement nevertheless.

When they had got past the initial burst of excitement, they both flopped down onto the dining room chairs and marvelled again at the note, and passed the key backwards and forwards between them, imagining what it might be for. Because of course, neither of them knew. They decided to keep it safe because it looked very old, and they wondered whether perhaps it was for another chest or trunk in the attic which the Fynd wanted to make sure they could get into.

Chapter 11

Scientific observations

Most of the rest of that warm July day was taken up with the wonder of what or who had been discovered at Willow Beck.

Freddie and Granny P read the Fynd's entry in Grandpa P's book so many times that Freddie began to remember whole sentences from it in his head.

And just before lunch he decided it would be a good idea to make a sort of booklet of the most important points so that Granny P and he could remember them, and keep them easily to hand in one of the sideboard drawers.

Freddie was very scientific in his approach.

Now he was convinced the Fynd was real, he wanted to study it and learn as much about its habits and nature as possible. He was also secretly hoping that if he found out a lot about the Fynd, he would be able to care for it very well... and it might become friends with him, and perhaps even let him catch a glimpse of it.

Then he, Freddie Perkins – the latest in a long line of explorers – would be the first person to ever see the Fynd properly.

* * *

His first efforts were focused on studying its food.

At lunch, he considered that the Fynd, who had eaten its breakfast a little while after theirs, might be hungry again by mid-afternoon, and so that would be a good time to conduct a study on which types of paper it would choose to eat.

Granny P and he speculated about possible paper delicacies over their own lunch of egg sandwiches and tomato soup.

'I imagine it would like soft paper, like tissues. Less effort to chew and better quality... rather like cake,' said Granny P with a wink.

'But wouldn't that be a bit stringy for it?' questioned Freddie. 'Perhaps it would prefer crunching through cardboard as if it were munching crisps?'

'Well, Freddie, as you say, the only way to find out is to conduct a proper, controlled experiment.'

And so they did.

When the lunch things had been cleared, they laid out as many different types of paper as possible. There was standard wrapping paper, foil wrapping paper, glitter paper, white cardboard, corrugated cardboard, cereal packet, newspaper, magazine paper, tissue paper, hand-made paper, posh watercolour paper, toilet roll, kitchen towel, and even some crepe paper which Freddie had found upstairs.

Granny P managed to find a piece of Indian silk paper which she was kindly going to add. But Freddie saw her face was a little sad and realised just in time that it might be special to her. He didn't want to let on to Granny P that he'd realised she might mind, so instead, he said he was a bit worried that silk, as it was a different fibre, would be poisonous for the Fynd, or simply too difficult to digest, and so probably not worth the risk of including.

And then Freddie made up a mini-questionnaire to sit under all the different papers.

1. *Does this taste nice?*
2. *Is this texture OK for you?*
3. *Do you want more of this?*

Freddie then labelled all the samples, and counted them. There were fourteen different types of paper and he was a bit concerned that there was too much for the Fynd to get through in one meal.

He wanted it to be able to focus on chewing the contents of the experiment rather than anything else, so he decided to save some of its appetite by asking Granny P to make a whole stack of scraps of paper with ticks and crosses on, so the Fynd wouldn't have to chew its answers.

Freddie and Granny P worked hard for at least an hour, preparing the experiment. Finally, they were content that it was the perfect test.

Again they left the dining room, only this time they made the wait less agonising by going for a walk through the garden, and down the hill towards the loch.

* * *

Freddie was so excited to be back near the house, and to be so close to the results of his first official Fynd study. But Granny P was finding it slow going up the hill, and eventually he could wait no longer. She smiled at him, and as if sensing his carefully held-in impatience, said 'Freddie, you go ahead and find out the results. Then you can present your findings just like all scientists do!'

'Thanks, Granny P!' he yelled over his shoulder, for he had started running ahead the moment she had begun to say he could.

Freddie ran up the hill, through the garden, up the path, into the entrance hall, and then paused at the dining room door.

He realised his mistake, too late of course... he should have come in quietly, tip-toeing into the house, because then he might have surprised the Fynd in the middle of its feast.

'Oh well, next time,' he thought to himself, as he pushed the slightly-ajar-door fully open and walked purposefully into the room to survey his results.

'No way!' he exclaimed.

There was nothing left! The Fynd had eaten everything. Ticks, crosses, questionnaire and fourteen different paper samples!

The only exceptions were three tiny scraps of newspaper print laid out in order to read

Freddie sunk down onto one of the dining room chairs, still breathless from his run.

How could you study something if it wouldn't obey the rules?

* * *

When Granny P joined Freddie in the dining room she took in the scene and its implications at once. And as usual, she had thought of something wonderful that Freddie hadn't even considered.

'What a delightful discovery,' she said. 'The Fynd likes things best that have print on them, so it can communicate. I think it wants to be friends with us, Freddie!'

Freddie felt all his disappointment at the thought-to-have-failed experiment fall away as a rush of excitement took its place.

'What do you think it will tell us, Granny P?'

Granny P smiled at him, and then gave him a playful poke. 'Well, there's only one way to find out.'

'What, *now*? Surely it can't possibly eat anything else after all that paper?'

'It does seem to be asking for more, Freddie... let's give it a try.'

So they did.

They split up to better cover the house and found as much newspaper as they could from packing crates in the attic, the waste-paper bin in Dad's study, and the recycling stack by the back door.

Between them they constructed a massive pile of it on the dining room table. Freddie was a bit worried that it wasn't safe to leave so much all at once, in case the Fynd ate all of that too and made itself ill. But Granny P said she had a feeling it just wanted to do things on its own terms, and they should trust it to be responsible.

For the third and final time that day they backed out of the dining room, leaving the door just slightly open, and retreating quietly to leave the space free for the Fynd and its paper.

The wait this time was sat out in the sitting room, and Freddie found it unbearably long.

He wasn't exactly surprised that Granny P fell asleep only ten minutes in, because they had had such an exciting and exhausting day. But all the same it was hard because now he didn't even have anyone to talk to him to help pass the time.

He couldn't settle to anything.

He tried reading his favourite comic, watching TV, and playing computer games, but somehow none of their made-up worlds captivated his interest half as much as what he now knew was going on just across the hall.

This was the kind of agonising waiting time that only drawing could fill, and he even got as far as getting out his sketchpad and pencils. But it was no good, the ideas just wouldn't come like they used to.

There was nothing for it. He would simply have to sit it out.

* * *

At two minutes before five, when the hour was not quite entirely up, but Freddie's patience absolutely was, he woke Granny P. Despite her nap, she was as impatient as him to see what the Fynd had said, and so they both rushed into the dining room.

There on the table were more words – quite a lot more than the two short phrases they had seen so far.

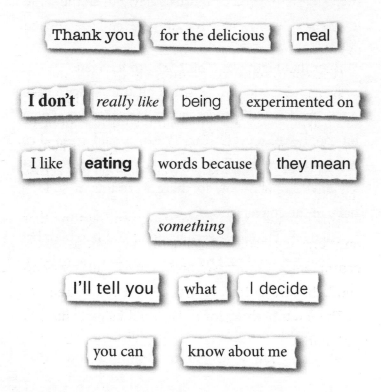

Thank you for the delicious meal

I don't *really like* being experimented on

I like **eating** words because they mean

something

I'll tell you what I decide

you can know about me

'Wow!' said Freddie, 'Wow!'

Granny P was just about to say that she could think of no other word for it when the front door shut and Dad called out that he was home.

Nothing more needed to be said. Granny P and Freddie quickly tidied up the pieces of paper into Freddie's earlier created 'Fynd studies' folder, and hid it in the sideboard drawer with the booklet he had made about taking care of the Fynd.

* * *

Dinner that night was a bit tricky to navigate.

Dad and Freddie were still a bit uneasy with each other. And Freddie and Granny P were struggling a bit too, because everything that was said seemed to remind them of the Fynd. But of course they couldn't say anything about it, so there were lots of sudden halts in the conversation.

All in all, Freddie was relieved to go up to bed that night so he could just relax and go over the magical day in his head.

But as he lay there, revelling in the excitement of it, he couldn't help but still feel sad about his dad.

He didn't know how he or Granny P could ever

explain to him that they had a Fynd in the house, and without an explanation, how could he ever break through the silence that was back between them since the terrible row?

Exhausted from trying so hard to conjure up a solution, he fell asleep. But his dreams were full of treasure hunts and chewed up paper words floating around, and strange, mythical creatures from Grandpa P's book.

Chapter 12

Find and seek

The next morning, Freddie woke up to the sound of his door being gently shut. He turned over towards his bedside table thinking that Granny P must have brought him a drink in bed, and left it next to the genie teapot. But there was nothing there besides the pot itself.

Freddie half sat up slowly, rubbing the sleep from his eyes as he did so, and looking around the room puzzled, and still half asleep.

It was then that he saw it.

Over in the right-hand back corner of his room, near his desk, his waste-paper bin had been knocked over and some of its contents spilled out on the floor. 'How did that happen?' he wondered.

Now he was properly awake.

He sat up straight, and pulled back the curtain nearest to him, letting the bright July morning into his room. What was that behind the bin? It looked like some kind of book... and what was his glue stick doing off the shelf and on the floor?

Barely three seconds had passed before Freddie was up, over in the corner, and down on his knees to investigate. Who had put it there?

He gasped with excitement as he looked at its cover. The book was large, heavy and beautifully bound. Freddie didn't know for certain if it was leather, but it felt like it might be. Was it a record of more of his family's historic adventures?

But as he hurriedly opened the book, he frowned in frustration. It was empty – and not at all old, as its cover had suggested. It was just a blank scrapbook.

He flicked through a few of the clean, fresh smelling pages and saw square after square of inviting space waiting to be filled with beautiful pictures, or magical stories, or personal memoirs, and quickly he began to feel excited again. What would he use it for? It would have to be filled with something wonderful because it was that kind of book.

Freddie was lost to his creative plans for a few minutes so he wasn't quite sure which came first – the remembrance that it was still a mystery how the book had got to his room, or the flicking to the front inside cover. But either way, question and answer became one as he read four simple words, constructed carefully and neatly from chewed up newsprint, and glued near the middle of the page as if they were a dedication.

Freddie put his hands to his head and fell sideways in an almost comical gesture of exaggerated frustration. 'No way!' he said 'I don't believe it... it must have been *right here!*'

The idea that the Fynd had come in with a massive book, knocked over the bin to access the newspaper in there, had a good square meal, and then merrily chewed out a message and neatly stuck it on to the page *all while he was asleep* was just too much for Freddie.

'Unbelievable! I missed it again!'

He sank on to the bed despondently.

After a while though, he began to laugh.

It was an amazing gift, and the Fynd must be feeling so smug that it had managed to do all that without waking him. Yet again it had eluded him. And it was so brilliant to have such a wonderful book to record everything in.

He couldn't wait to show it to Granny P – how she would laugh! Oh, and he supposed that he'd better check it was OK for him to have it – after all, the Fynd had found it, but it had probably belonged to Granny P all along.

Freddie snatched up the book and began to run out of his room and downstairs to find her. He felt exhilarated by the possibilities of what they could put in the book, and by the joy of having such a brilliant thing to tell Granny P about.

Where was she?

He ran first to the sitting room, and then into the kitchen, and then back into the entrance hall, getting more and more excited, and then...

He ran straight into his dad. Without thinking, he flung his arms round him, sending the book to the floor with an impressive thump, and blurting out his excitement in a hurry.

'Dad, Dad, where's Granny P? The most brilliant thing has happened. And I've found this amazing journal, and I need to find her, and I want to check it's OK for me to have it, and I... Dad... Dad?'

Freddie broke off, for after hugging him back strongly, his dad had suddenly seemed to stiffen, and then to disengage. It was then that Freddie remembered, of course, that things were still not really right between them.

He felt the silence begin to descend as he stepped back away from his dad, embarrassed now that he had forgotten, and disappointed too that his dad couldn't just let it go. It had felt so right for just a second there, to hug his dad like old times again.

But Freddie's dad wasn't breaking away from him. Instead, he was going over to the book and kneeling down by it.

Freddie moved to join him, half intrigued as to why his dad was so interested in it, and half worried that his dad would ask questions about the dedication that might lead to another fight.

Tentatively, he placed a hand on his dad's shoulder as he stood next to him to see what he was looking at. And that was when he discovered that Dad wasn't looking at the book at all, but at a picture that had fallen out of it of a beautiful young woman holding a tiny baby.

Even standing just to the right and behind of him, Freddie could see that there were tears on Dad's cheeks. He realised it must be his mum and him in the picture.

'Oh Freddie,' said his dad shakily. 'I miss her so much.'

Freddie was a little scared because Dad was so big and strong and never cried, and he felt the silence muscling in and elbowing him out completely.

And so he took himself out of the equation, walking past his dad and towards the doorway back into the sitting room. But when he turned to look back at him, and the faraway look in his eyes, he noticed some writing on the back of the photo.

'Dad!' he cried out. 'Dad, there's some of Mum's writing on the back!'

In a second, Freddie and his dad were back together, looking at the reverse of the photo, and reading the wonderful words of a note that was as old as Freddie himself, but as new to them as if Mum had just written it today, and left it somewhere for her 'two favourite boys' to find and read, just like old times.

Dear Pa,

Here as promised is the very first picture of our latest Perkins man! Isn't he splendid?!

My copy of it is of course going in the beautiful frame you carved for that very purpose. Thank you again – I love it!

I can't wait to see how this little one's story is going to read and develop. But if he's anything as brave, and loving, and good, and kind as Stephen is, then I know you and I will be just as proud of him as we all are of your son.

I'm looking forward so much to when Freddie's old enough to hear all about the mysterious creatures in and around Willow Beck - I hope he loves hearing your stories as much as I do.

I was so inspired this last time, I've been doing a drawing of how I imagine one of them. I'll leave which one as a surprise until I next see you! But it's got me thinking, perhaps we could use this book to put them together with your stories for Ma, and for Freddie when he is older.

What do you think? I know Ma would be so happy if you finally got round to doing this too!

With much love

Amie

Somehow, Freddie just knew this note was what the Fynd had really been leading him to.

And just as he was wondering what to do, and whether he should break the wonder of this moment by explaining that he knew the very picture mentioned in the note, the wind was almost knocked out of him as his dad reached his arm round him, and propelled him inwards, into the fiercest bear hug Freddie had ever experienced.

The silence shattered into a thousand pieces.

And Freddie and his dad stood in the hallway at Willow Beck and held on to each other so tightly it almost hurt.

Chapter 13

Seeing the full picture

A few minutes later, Freddie took his dad up to his bedroom to show him the drawing in the wooden frame. They sat on Freddie's bed together, his dad holding the photo with the note, and Freddie holding the picture in the frame.

'She was so amazing, wasn't she, Dad?'

'Yes, Freddie, she was.'

'I... I...' stuttered Freddie. 'I found this again the other day when we... I mean when I... it really helped me when I was on my own up here and thinking and, well, you know... and I wanted to say thank you for it again, that you gave it to me and didn't just keep it for yourself, I mean.'

'I wanted you to have it. And Mum would have wanted that too. She was so proud of your drawing. She used to tell me you were so much better than she was at your age.'

'Really?' said Freddie. 'She never told me that.'

'Didn't want it to go to your head, probably,' said Dad, giving him a nudge.

Freddie giggled, but then went quiet again.

'I haven't really been able to draw... since...'

'You will be able to again, Freddie. I promise. I don't know when, but you'll start again. Maybe you need something particular to inspire you. Shall we ask your grandmother if she has any ideas?'

Freddie remembered Granny P in a rush. 'Oh brilliant, yes! Granny P will know where I should start. Oh Dad, I still haven't asked her about the book, and we need to show it to her! And the photo... and the note... and, well, we should probably tell her we've talked.'

'Yes, you're right. You go and show her everything while I make her a cup of tea and then come and join you. I don't actually think she's up yet – it was still pretty early when you were careering around downstairs!'

* * *

Freddie knocked on Granny P's door, sat beside her bed as instructed, and then proceeded to whisper to her – just in case Dad suddenly came back – the story of how the book had come into his possession in the first place.

Then he showed her the marvellous dedication at the front of it.

Granny P was delighted with this latest find, and said that of course Freddie should have it. She thought it was absolutely wonderful that the Fynd had been so close to him all that time, but totally understood his frustration that once again it had given him the slip.

But then she got caught up in the book itself again.

'It's strange, Freddie, but I don't remember ever seeing this, and it's obviously come from the main house rather than the attic, wouldn't you say?'

By way of explanation Freddie handed her the photo of him and his mum note-side up. 'Dad and I found this inside it, Granny P. I guess Grandpa P was keeping it a secret from you until it was ready.'

Granny P read the note, and looked at the image, and seemed a little bit choked up, so Freddie was relieved when Dad came in with the tea at that point, and she posed her next question to him.

'Stephen, do you remember how I was always trying to persuade your father to write down his stories? Isn't it wonderful that he and Amie were going to do that for me? And for Freddie too. Imagine them keeping it all a surprise...' Granny P's smile faded slightly, as she thought back to that time.

'How very sad that Reg died so soon after that. They must have never had the chance.'

Freddie handed Granny P the picture then. 'I found this just the other night Granny P, look. This is the one Mum had already drawn.'

'Oh, but isn't that beautiful. What a way that girl had of capturing things.'

'Dad and I were just saying that!' said Freddie, smiling at Granny P, and then up at his dad, who had come over to stand next to him and was resting a hand gently on his shoulder.

Granny P looked at her son and grandson, and the unspoken conversation which was passing between them, and her whole face lit up, but she said nothing.

Instead, she hastily got up, mumbled something about getting ready for Mrs Quinn, and then left the room and them in it.

Freddie and his dad laughed. It was obvious she wanted to give them more time together without making a fuss. But it was *so* obvious that it made them giggle uncontrollably.

* * *

Freddie and his dad cuddled up on Granny P's big bed, looking at the picture and the photo some more, chatting companionably and then at last falling into a comfortable quietness with each other. After some time, Dad suddenly sat up straight.

'Freddie!' he said 'Why didn't I think of it before? I know what we can do. You and I will do it. We'll fill the book for Granny P. Don't tell her, but I remember all Grandpa's stories – I heard them so many times growing up, Freddie! And you can do the drawings. Do you think you could start drawing for something like this? We could work on it together in secret and then give it to her when it's ready. What do you reckon?'

Freddie just smiled.

He was a bit nervous about the drawing, of course. But he so wanted to do something wonderful for Granny P, and he supposed that somehow it might help him overcome the block in his mind that wouldn't let him draw what was hidden in there.

'That's settled, then,' said Dad. 'We'll begin right away. Now, Pa's favourite story of all was – I warn you – a ridiculously far-fetched one about a creature he swore was called "the Fynd"... you'll laugh at this one. Where shall I start?'

And Freddie did laugh at the story, but of course, it wasn't for the reason his dad thought.

Chapter 14

More Fynd studies

The next couple of weeks were packed full as July raced into August.

There was still sorting in the attic, of course, but now there were new discoveries to make about the Fynd, new things constantly being found by it to look out for, and of course drawing. For now Freddie had started again, he could hardly stop. And he found he was often torn between working in secret on the book for Granny P, helping her with the sorting of more exciting things in the attic, and responding to the objects and notes that the Fynd was finding and leaving for them.

It was wonderful to be drawing again. In the end, the solution had been easy. Dad had suggested he begin by copying Mum's sketch, so they could have it on the front cover as well as inside the book when they worked out which creature it might go next to.

And as he copied her work, it was almost as if she was there again, translating the complex life captured on the page into easily manageable shapes, lines and measurements. His attempt wasn't at all bad, though he could tell the head was somehow out of proportion. But he imagined Mum saying it was an improvement on hers, just to be nice – though it wasn't, of course.

Dad seemed genuinely impressed, saying he thought Freddie was getting better and better, and then taking him out to buy some grown-up pastels, which he thought would suit the style Freddie was now developing.

Just as it had promised, the Fynd had been leaving various notes for Freddie and Granny P to help them with their studies of it. So far these had mostly been about paper and its seemingly endless appetite for it. But Granny P was hoping that it would soon tell them more about where it came from, how long it had been at Willow Beck for, and whether it had known Grandpa P.

It found other ways to spell out its opinions too. For example, it wasn't long before patterns began to emerge in response to certain kinds of print. The Fynd seemed to spit out some sections, almost as if they tasted bad, while whole other sections of the paper would disappear incredibly quickly. And then there were some portions which inspired a specific 'thank' 'you' in the customary manner.

It was baffling at first, because of course it was all the same type of paper. But after hours of speculation, and analysing the rejected regurgitations, Granny P worked it out – the Fynd only had an appetite for good news. Marriage and birth announcements seemed to be a particularly satisfying meal, whilst critical, angry or just plain mean stories were spat out in what, Granny P supposed, must be disgust.

Granny P found the whole thing amazing, but Freddie continued to be frustrated as well as excited by the gradual discovery process.

There were the notes of course, but it still seemed to be much more interested in finding things than in revealing itself. Almost every evening there was a new object from Dad's childhood to show him, or a piece of some new great-great-grandparent's history.

Freddie would have rather it concentrated on his studies of it, thoroughly and logically. He wanted to map it all out methodically, moving from one area of study to the next, in order to build up proof and conclusive findings of the Fynd's existence and habits. Then they would have enough evidence to tell Dad.

Instead, the Fynd seemed to prefer mystery, and to have what Granny P described as 'a flair for the dramatic'. It was still keeping a secret all the things that really *mattered* to Freddie – like what it looked like, how big it was, and whether it would ever let him meet it face to face.

* * *

One Tuesday morning Freddie decided he could wait no longer. He would simply have to take matters into his own hands.

He chatted his ideas over with Granny P of course, but this time she refused to be involved in his experiments.

'I don't think it works like that, Freddie,' she warned. 'I really think you should be careful. The Fynd has made it clear what its terms are, and you might find there are consequences to trying to get round it.'

But Freddie was insistent that he had to try, and that the Fynd wouldn't find out what he was doing anyway.

Granny P looked uncomfortable but said nothing more.

* * *

Freddie laid out an inviting spread of newspaper stories, called out loudly (as if to Granny P) that he was going into the garden, and then quietly crept across to the sideboard.

The main space inside it was very large and Freddie had prepared it well, clearing it out and sorting old piles of things with the well-practised expertise of one who had conquered almost an entire attic of yesterdays in a single summer.

Silently he climbed into the left-hand side of it, putting his legs down and round behind the dividing support that semi-separated the space into two areas, and stretching them out as far as was possible into the half that was behind the closed, right-hand door. And then, still uncomfortable but in, he twisted on his side awkwardly in order to pull the left-hand door almost closed.

He reached down to where his camera was hung around his neck, got it out, pointed it through the thin stripe of light, and waited.

And waited... and waited.

But the only things he managed to prove conclusively were that you got really painful neck ache from lying in such a cramped space for so long, and a bumped head if you sat up suddenly in response to an unexpected noise in the room you were hiding in.

It was just Granny P.

Freddie sighed in disappointment. Clearly this way wasn't going to work.

He had to admit Granny P had been right, though it was slightly galling to come back downstairs for lunch, having only been gone from the dining room for ten minutes, and discover that all the tempting tit-bit stories had been eaten but for two words –

'Aaaaggh! But when am I going to get to see *you*?' cried Freddie out loud.

But the only response he got was from Granny P, who was carrying in a pot of macaroni cheese, and asked him who he was talking to.

* * *

Freddie was a bit sulky over lunch that day. Even though macaroni cheese was one of his favourite meals, and Granny P was chatting away to him excitedly about various things that she'd found in the attic that morning.

He tried to look as interested as he could, but his mind was working overtime on how he could trick the Fynd into being seen.

And then suddenly, he registered something

Granny P had been saying, and had a brilliant – beyond brilliant – idea.

'Granny P?' he asked. 'Did you say you'd found an old video camera?'

'Yes Freddie. Why? Would you like it?' she asked, 'I don't know how it works, but it looks hardly used, and there's an instruction book with it. Your mum gave it to Reg for his birthday one year, but he never managed to work out how to use it, poor love. You're good with all that sort of thing though, aren't you? Yes, have it, Freddie. It would be fun to make some films. It's a shame we couldn't have had that right from the start of sorting the attic, because then we could have filmed one of those before and after programmes your dad likes.'

Granny P laughed at her own cleverness, but Freddie had drifted off again. Yes, he wanted the video camera. And yes, he was sure he could work out how to use it with the instruction book.

* * *

That afternoon Freddie helped Granny P with the attic, and then, just before six, he took the video camera downstairs. After dinner, while Granny P and Dad chatted happily to each other from their respective chairs in the sitting room, Freddie lay on the floor and pored over the instruction book.

This was the solution for sure.

At bedtime he put a choice selection of magazines and comics onto the dining room table, and left the camera and its instructions carefully and quietly on the sideboard, ready to enact part two of his brilliant plan.

He lay in bed, keeping himself awake in the dark by imagining all the different shapes and sizes that the Fynd might be, and occasionally pinching himself when he was near to dropping off.

Once he'd heard Dad's door shut for the final time he counted slowly to three hundred to be sure, and then he crept downstairs.

He was seriously impressed with himself. Willow Beck was an old house and it had creaky floorboards, squeaky doors and a hundred other make-a-noise traps like that which gave your presence away. But he had got to know most of them now, and was handling the stealth operation expertly. He managed to get all the way into the dining room without making the slightest noise externally. (Internally of course his heart was banging a wildly staccato drum beat, but not even the Fynd could hear that.)

Freddie approached the sideboard and his hands felt for the camera. He switched it on, knowing its screen would provide enough light for him to read the final instructions and leave it running for the night.

He swung the camera to the right to begin.

But there were no instructions there.

Just four words, chewed neatly and precisely.

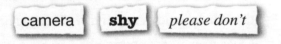

For some reason Freddie didn't feel cross or frustrated when he read this.

Instead, a kind of impressed acceptance descended into him as he stood there in the camera's glow, reading the Fynd's latest note.

It was simply too smart for him. He couldn't outwit it. And he supposed that was quite wonderful after all. It was more important that it was here, and staying, than that he got to see it in any case. Maybe Granny P was right – some things were more magical if they remained mysteries.

Freddie cleared up the words, and took them and the camera upstairs, still creeping slowly so as not to wake Dad and Granny P, though he now realised that even the stealthiest tracking methods would not prevent the Fynd from knowing he was up in the middle of the night.

Chapter 15

Finding and keeping

From the day after the camera incident, Freddie stopped trying to trick the Fynd or capture proof of it, and simply enjoyed caring for it, and continuing to receive its notes when they came.

He put out paper three times a day (Granny P started ordering extra newspapers and magazines so the Fynd would always have plenty, and sometimes Freddie would add an old birthday card from a relative, or a friendly postcard from one of his old school friends in London, as he imagined these would make the Fynd especially happy). One set of paper was laid out in the morning just after breakfast, one at lunchtime while Granny P was preparing their food, and a final set when she was making dinner, before Dad usually came home.

They didn't tell Freddie's dad about their discovery, because paper disappearing and strange notes made from chewed-up newsprint by way of proof were almost as crazy as the problem of things appearing where you didn't leave them. But between them they developed a secret code of simply smiling and nodding on the few occasions Dad noticed items that belonged to him suddenly appear. They didn't want to lie to him, or to take credit for something they hadn't done, but they didn't feel quite ready to just come out with it either.

Over those last, busy days of the school holidays, more precious or simply lost items turned up in the house. And more and more of the attic became clear and tidy until the huge space was almost empty.

The diaries were with the curator of the local museum who was studying and researching the accounts they contained (he had also taken the newspapers, various photos and some very old documents to look at) and Campbell and Sons had taken the necklace to be auctioned in Edinburgh. Granny P was hopeful that the proceeds from its sale would be enough to level out a section of the garden so that Freddie could play football more easily, and have a small flat area where they could lay tarmac and put up a hoop.

All of the antiques they had found had gone to experts to value. All the interesting or beautiful things they wanted to keep had been found new homes in the main house. And bags and bags of rubbish, or things they simply didn't want, had been cleared out into the recycling bins, bags for the charity shops or the small skip Granny P had been forced to order.

* * *

It was the last day of the school holidays, with a perfect August display of sunshine and blue skies. But Granny P and Freddie were going to spend the morning inside, finishing off in the attic, whilst Dad was at the auction house negotiating the sale of a few last bits and pieces.

They had been spurred on by a promise from Dad.

'If you two workers are done by the time I get back,' he'd said with a wink, 'I'll take the three of us out for a special surprise treat.'

And that had done it. Freddie could have sworn even Granny P had moved reasonably quickly in response, and he had practically sprinted up the stairs himself. It was hard to know which of them was more eager and excited to finish it, and find out what Dad had planned for them.

A little while later, as they surveyed the now empty space, Granny P sighed. 'Freddie, I'm sorry, I still can't figure out what that key is for. It's very strange.'

'Never mind Granny P,' said Freddie with a smile. 'There have been so many mysteries this summer. One more won't hurt.'

Granny P chuckled. 'Now we can get to them, Freddie, let's clean up these windows and find out just how far we can see from all the way up here.'

Freddie protested at this, because no boy his age wants to clean windows, especially on the last day of their holidays, and so Granny P relented. He had been so helpful all summer. She had to admit this was fair enough.

'You win,' she said. 'Why don't you go and do something more fun while I clean them?'

But Freddie discovered he didn't really want to do that either. It looked like hard work, and Granny P was old. So he said that he would help after all, and they should start at one end each and meet in the middle.

Freddie scrubbed and scrubbed what he could reach of his windows, but all he could see, because of their angle and his height, was sky. He tried jumping up and down to catch a glimpse of it, but it was no good. He couldn't see anything else.

When they reached the middle Granny P insisted on doing the fifth and final window so he could go and get a footstool from downstairs to stand on and look out from.

Freddie was excited. Soon he would get to see out of the windows. It was ages since he had had such a high-up view.

Not since Westgate Square Gardens, in fact.

He bounded down the steps two at a time, and stopped dead.

Because it was then that he saw it.

It was sitting on the bottom step of the stairs. Small, brown, and hunched over what he could only guess was some paper. It was slightly furry, but not cuddly looking, with long arms and legs (the latter dangling over the bottom step) and a long tail.

It reminded Freddie of something he'd seen before. But he didn't have time to consider what. For, before he could examine it more closely, it heard him approaching.

It was gone in a flash.

But Freddie knew what, or rather who, it was.

He had seen the Fynd!

OK, only from behind. But the book had said no one had seen one properly. No one. If he could only just see its face!

He stood rooted to the spot. He didn't know what to do. He didn't know where the Fynd was hiding, and whether talking to it, or chasing after it, would frighten it.

But then, he wanted to see its face so much. And he did need to get the footstool.

Freddie made up his mind. He would go down the final few stairs onto the landing. And so, cautiously, he edged down the staircase, trying to be as gentle and quiet as he could be. And then he crept round the corner...

... and there it was again.

It was sitting at the top of the next flight down to the bedrooms below.

Freddie hesitated. Moving closer seemed like it would only scare it again, and so he sat down some distance away, as quietly as he could, and waited. Perhaps, if it became aware of his presence, it would run again, but perhaps it might turn as it did so, and he would get to see its face.

He waited and waited. And the Fynd sat and sat.

And then the impossible happened.

The Fynd slowly shifted position and turned round towards him.

It had the kindest, wisest face he had ever seen. Beautifully lined, and the colour of parchment paper. And its deep, dark eyes looked at him with more understanding than he had ever known.

But it did not smile.

It looked... well, sad.

And strangely familiar. The picture! It was really like the picture! Not exactly the same – that was why he hadn't known straightaway – but it was *very* like it.

And then, with a sudden movement, it was gone – downstairs again.

Freddie went down after it. Slowly, slowly, slowly. But there was no sign of it at all. Not at the bottom of those stairs, nor the next... and anyway, it could have gone in any direction by now.

Freddie sighed. He was disappointed.

But then he rallied. He had seen the Fynd! He had seen its *face*!

Perhaps it was the first step to them becoming real friends. If the Fynd had been seen once and not been terrified – which he was sure it hadn't been, from the way it had looked – then it might not mind being seen again, and maybe for longer this time.

But why was the Fynd sad?

Granny P might know, he thought. Granny P was surely as wise and kind as the Fynd. She would know.

Freddie felt better immediately. He could ask Granny P and she would be sure to help. He'd just get the footstool – she'd probably been wondering why he was taking so long – then he'd go up and ask. Mind you, wouldn't she be amazed that the Fynd absolutely, undeniably was real? And that he, Freddie Perkins, a modern-day explorer, had seen its face...

And – he realised it in a flash – he must not have been the first one to do so, after all!

He hoped Granny P wouldn't be too disappointed that she hadn't seen it yet. He was sure they would see it again. Maybe even at dinner tonight.

Freddie ran to his room to get the footstool, but then stopped short. Because on the footstool he was moving towards was a piece of paper with lots of chewed-out newspaper words on. Freddie fell on his knees to read it.

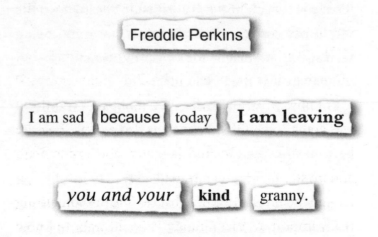

Freddie Perkins

I am sad because today **I am leaving**

you and your **kind** granny.

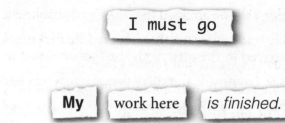

I must go

My work here *is finished.*

I have found you everything you need.

It was from the Fynd. It was going. It had probably already gone. He would never see it again.

And now he knew why the Fynd had shown itself to him. It was the final thing that it had revealed to him before it left – the truth that he wasn't the only one to have seen it.

The Fynd had helped them find so many things, but more than anything it had helped him find Granny P – to know who she really was, and that everything was going to be OK. To find his dad again. To come back to drawing. To find laughter, and excitement, and mysteries, and secrets, and... life.

And today it had allowed him to find out something really important that Granny P would want to know about. Freddie wanted to tell her right now.

* * *

Freddie arrived in the attic with the footstool just in time to see Granny P perched precariously on her tiptoes. She was looking intently into the distance through the far left corner of the far left window, and wiping a tear or two away from her eyes.

He put down the stool and ran over to her, throwing his arms round her frail body and holding on like he would never let go.

'I love you, Granny,' he said.

'I know, Freddie,' she said. 'I love you too.'

After a few moments, Granny P said, 'Come on then, quickly, get the footstool. You must see the view we have worked so hard to find.'

So Freddie did. He put it under the central gable window, and carefully climbed up on to it so he could finally see out.

'Wow!' he cried 'This is such an awesome view. Wow! I can see the loch and everything and I...'

'And I what?'

'I don't have words, Granny. It's so beautiful.'

'I thought we might try pictures. Like you and your mum used to do.'

Freddie felt the familiar lump, but this time he let it come. One slow, quiet tear rolled down his cheek and he looked at Granny P.

'I think Mum would have loved us to do that... and Dad too. It would make Dad really happy.'

Granny P smiled and hugged him again – which was a funny experience because he was now a lot taller than her because of the stool.

'This would make a wonderful studio for you, Freddie,' she said. 'And base-camp for preparing more studies and experiments...'

'Oh,' he said, and his heart dropped, because he hated that he was going to have say it out loud. 'Granny, the Fynd... well, I saw it, and... it's gone now.'

'I know, Freddie,' said his granny, giving him another squeeze. 'I was so impatient to see the view that I was standing on tiptoes trying to glimpse something. And I was doing it just at the right moment because I saw it all the way from up here – even though it was so tiny. It turned and waved. I was sure somehow that it would have said goodbye to you too.'

'Did you see it close enough to see what its face looked like?'

'No, I didn't.'

'It was really like Mum's picture. Not exactly the same, of course, because Mum never saw it, just heard it described. But don't you see what this means, Granny? Grandpa P must have seen the Fynd too!'

Granny P's whole face lit up but she didn't say anything else, just hugged him even closer to her.

And they stood like that for a long time, the boy and the old lady, in the empty attic, where the Fynd had helped them to find everything they needed.

* * *

Our story ends here. Not because this is the end for Freddie, Granny P, Dad and life at Willow Beck. Their story is just beginning now. So many adventures lie ahead of the Perkins family – after all, they still have to find what that other key is for.

But our story ends here because the Fynd has gone. And so we must go too, to search for where it has gone, and who and what it will help find next.

About the Author

Liz Baddaley lives a life surrounded by words, whether they're for the children's novels she has begun to create, or for the leading UK charities she writes for. Liz was born in St Albans and read English at Christ Church, Oxford, but is now most likely to be found tapping away at her laptop with a pot of tea, or exploring Ilkley's famous moor - singing along to her iPod and desperately trying to keep up with Rabbit the dog.